T[...]
BILLIONA[...]
by P[...]
meet Forrest Cunningham—
cattle baron of The Golden Steer.
When deciding to settle down,
Forrest gets more than he bargained for with
Becky Sullivan—
a tomboy all grown up who wants more than a
duty-bound marriage pact!

**SILHOUETTE DESIRE
IS PROUD TO PRESENT THE**

Five wealthy Texas bachelors—all members
of the state's most exclusive club—set out on a
mission to rescue a princess…and find true love.

* * *

And don't miss SECRET AGENT DAD by
Metsy Hingle, next month's installment of the
Texas Cattleman's Club, available in
Silhouette Desire!

Dear Reader,

Welcome to Silhouette Desire—where you're guaranteed powerful, passionate and provocative love stories that feature rugged heroes and spirited heroines who experience the full emotional intensity of falling in love!

This October you'll love our new MAN OF THE MONTH title by Barbara Boswell, *Forever Flint*. Opposites attract when a city girl becomes the pregnant bride of a millionaire outdoorsman.

Be sure to "rope in" the next installment of the exciting Desire miniseries TEXAS CATTLEMAN'S CLUB with *Billionaire Bridegroom* by Peggy Moreland. When cattle baron Forrest Cunningham wants to wed childhood friend Becky Sullivan, she puts his love to an unexpected test.

The always-wonderful Jennifer Greene returns to Desire with her magical series HAPPILY EVER AFTER. *Kiss Your Prince Charming* is a modern fairy tale starring an unforgettable "frog prince." In a sexy battle-of-the-sexes tale, Lass Small offers you *The Catch of Texas*. Anne Eames continues her popular miniseries MONTANA MALONES with *The Unknown Malone*. And Sheri WhiteFeather makes her explosive Desire debut with *Warrior's Baby,* a story of surrogate motherhood with a twist.

Next month, you'll really feel the power of the passion when you see our new provocative cover design. Underneath our new covers, you will still find six exhilarating journeys into the seductive world of romance, with a guaranteed happy ending!

Enjoy!

Joan Marlow Golan
Senior Editor, Silhouette Desire

Please address questions and book requests to:
Silhouette Reader Service
U.S.: 3010 Walden Ave., P.O. Box 1325, Buffalo, NY 14269
Canadian: P.O. Box 609, Fort Erie, Ont. L2A 5X3

BILLIONAIRE BRIDEGROOM
PEGGY MORELAND

SILHOUETTE *Desire*®

Published by Silhouette Books

America's Publisher of Contemporary Romance

To Dixie, Jen, Metsy and Cindy, who share with me the distinction of being
the only females to gain entrance to the exclusive Texas Cattleman's Club—
other than Miss Manie, of course. It's been fun, ladies. Let's do this again!

Special thanks to Mr. and Mrs. Larry Hunt of the H & B Cattle Company
in Monahans, Texas, for giving me a tour of their ranch and for so
generously sharing their knowledge of ranch life with me. And thanks,
too, to Jackie Youngblood, for her assistance in researching West Texas
and Wade County.

Special thanks and acknowledgment are given to
Peggy Moreland for her contribution to the
Texas Cattleman's Club miniseries.

SILHOUETTE BOOKS

RECYCLED PAPER

ISBN 0-373-76244-5

BILLIONAIRE BRIDEGROOM

Printed in U.S.A.

Books by Peggy Moreland

PEGGY MORELAND

published her first romance with Silhouette in 1989. She's a natural storyteller with a sense of humor that will tickle your fancy, and Peggy's goal is to write a story that readers will remember long after the last page is turned. Winner of the 1992 National Readers' Choice Award and a 1994 RITA finalist, Peggy frequently appears on bestseller lists around the country. A native Texan, she and her family live in Round Rock, Texas.

"What's Happening in Royal?"

NEWS FLASH, October 1999—
Forrest Cunningham, owner of the prestigious cattle ranch The Golden Steer, is apparently trying to fulfill the marriage pact he made with next-door neighbor Becky Sullivan twelve years ago. Problem is, Ms. Sullivan seems to already have a fiancé, and a mystery one at that....

And a strange, rather aristocratic gentleman has been sighted walking about the town of Royal. Who could he be, and what does he want?

Our Texas Cattleman's Club members seem more secretive than ever.... What could be brewing?

Prologue

Royal, Texas, 1987

Sweat poured down Forrest Cunningham's face, plastered his shirt to his chest and back, and ran in rivulets down his spine, soaking the waist of his faded jeans a darker blue. After chasing steers through the scrub brush all afternoon under a hot West Texas sun, his boots—and his butt—were dragging as he led his horse to the rails of the corral.

Feeling as parched as the land he walked on, he dragged the back of his hand across his mouth and winced when grit scraped across his lips like coarse sandpaper. Thank goodness his partner on the roundup was an experienced wrangler, otherwise he was sure he'd have spewed cotton—and no words—if he'd been required to offer up any instruction. He was that dry.

With his thoughts focused on the beer iced down and waiting for him in a cooler propped on the tailgate, he tied his horse to the corral's top rail, then cut a quick path to the rear of the truck. He fished a cold brew from the cooler, popped the top, then, with a sigh of purest pleasure, lifted the beer.

"Hey, Woody! Wait! I get first sip!"

His mouth open and ready, his tongue and throat primed for that first thirst-quenching swig, Forrest considered pretending he hadn't heard Becky's request...but then he sighed and dutifully lowered the can. It was a ritual. Becky always got the first sip. And Forrest allowed it. Just as he allowed her to call him "Woody" and live to tell it. Five years his junior, and a neighbor for as long as he could remember, Becky Sullivan was like a kid sister to him and, as such, enjoyed full rights.

He angled his head, a grin tugging at the corner of his mouth, as he watched her charging toward him, her long legs churning, her hand flattened on the top of her battered cowboy hat to keep the wind from ripping it off her head. "You're too young to drink, kid," he called out to her. "You're only eighteen."

She skidded to a stop in front of him, snatched the can from his hand and shot him a scowl. "Yeah? So arrest me." She bumped the can against the brim of her hat, knocking it off, and thick red hair fell to pool around her shoulders. Lifting the beer in a silent toast, she shot Forrest a wink, then tipped back her head and drank deeply.

Forrest focused on the long, smooth column of her throat—and knew damn good and well he could kiss that beer goodbye. Becky Sullivan might be only eighteen, but she drank like a man, and held her liquor like one, too. He knew this for a fact because she'd drunk him under the table a time or two.

Truth be told, Becky could do most things as well as a man. She could outride, outrope and outshoot just about any male in Ward county. He supposed she'd learned these skills out of necessity, being as she'd pretty much raised herself and was responsible for whatever work was accomplished on her family's ranch, the Rusty Corral. The fact that he'd had a hand in teaching her a few of those skills brought a swell of pride. And the fact that she was a good student was why he'd sought her help today in rounding up some of his cattle rather than that of one of his own cowboys from the Golden Steer.

"Okay, brat," he muttered, wrestling the can from her grip. "Save some for me."

She backhanded the moisture from her mouth and grinned up at him. "You thirsty?"

"Damn straight." He tipped back his head and lifted the can, prepared to finish off the beer.

"Course you know," she added, "all that's left is backwash, but if you really want it—"

Beer spewed from Forrest's mouth. "Gawldangit, Becky," he complained, dragging a hand across his mouth. "Why'd you have to go and say that for?"

"Sorry," she said, though he could tell by the impish gleam in her eyes she wasn't one damn bit sorry. "Just thought I'd better warn you."

He chunked the empty can into the bed of his truck, then buried his hand in the cooler, searching for another beer. "Like I said. You're a brat." He fished out a new can from the cooler, turned—and immediately bumped against Becky's outstretched hand. With a resigned sigh, he tossed her the beer, then retrieved another for himself. After popping the top, he hooked an arm around her slim shoulders and headed her toward the shade provided by the trailer. "So where's your daddy gone this time?"

Her shoulder moved under his arm in a shrug. "Didn't say. Probably Riodoso, though. They're racing there this weekend."

Forrest plopped down beside the trailer, resting his back against its side and looked up at her. He'd figured it was horse racing, though Shorty Sullivan was never short on excuses for leaving the care of his ranch up to his young daughter…and her alone. "So you're batching?"

"Yep," Becky replied, dropping down next to him.

Shoulder to shoulder they stared out across the pasture, sipping their beers, while the cattle bawled pitifully in the corral, the silence between them a comfortable one.

"The Texas Cattleman's Ball is coming up in a couple of weeks," Becky offered after a bit.

Forrest pulled the brim of his hat over his eyes and settled in for a nap. "Yeah, it is."

"Who're you takin'?"

"Lyndean Sawyer from over in Midland."

"Haven't heard you mention her name before. She somebody new you're courtin'?"

Something in her voice made him nudge his hat from his eyes to peer at her. She was squinting hard at the sun, the corners of her mouth pulled down into a frown. "No. Just a date," he said slowly. When her frown deepened, he said, "Why do you ask?"

She lifted her beer, her movements tense and jerky, and took a sip. "Just curious."

"Are you going to the Ball this year?"

She pulled her spine away from the trailer, drawing her legs up, and draped an elbow over her knee as she squinted harder at something in the distance. "Nope."

"How come?"

"Nobody asked me."

Surprised by the splotch of red that suddenly appeared

on her cheeks, he gave her back a poke with his beer can.
"Oh, come on. Quit your foolin'. Surely someone has
asked you."

She angled her head far enough around to frown at him.
"No one has, and no one will, either."

"How can you be so sure?"

She turned away, setting her jaw. "Because I know.
That's how."

"A pretty girl like you? Boys'll be tripping all over
themselves for the chance to ask you to the Ball. Just you
wait and see."

As he stared at her, he was sure that he saw her chin
quiver. And were those tears making her eyes sparkle?
Naw, he told himself. Becky wasn't the crying type. Yet,
as he watched, a fat tear slipped over her lid and down
her cheek.

He tossed aside his beer and slung an arm around her
shoulder, drawing her against his side. "Aw, Becky.
Don't cry. The dance is still a couple of weeks away.
Somebody'll ask you."

She sniffed, dragging her sleeve beneath her nose, as
she pulled away from him. "Who? Billy Ray? Johnny?
They've already got dates." She gave her head a quick
shake, then pressed her cheek on her knee and began trac-
ing a path in the dirt with the tip of her finger. "No. No
one will ask me to the Ball. Maybe to head or heel for
them at the next roping competition, but never on a date."

Because he suspected what she said was probably true,
Forrest remained silent.

After a while, she lifted her head and turned to look at
him. "Woody, do you think I'll ever get married?"

The hopelessness in her voice touched his heart—and
made him a little uneasy. The word "marriage" always

had that effect on Forrest. He lifted a shoulder. "I don't know, Becky. I suppose you will, if you want to."

She turned her gaze to the pasture, squinting hard, as if in doing so she might be able to see into the future. "I don't think I will," she murmured after a long moment. "All the guys just think of me as one of them, never as a female." She choked back a laugh that sounded dangerously close to a sob. "I can see it now. Thirty years old, a dried-up old maid and still working the Rusty Corral all by myself."

Forrest dug his boot heels in the heat-dried grass, bringing himself alongside her. He looped an arm around her shoulders, and hugged her to his side. "Aw, now, Becky. It's not as bad as all that."

"No," she said miserably, "it's worse."

Forrest heard the defeat in her voice, as well as the loneliness. "Tell you what, Becky," he offered. "If you're not married by your thirtieth birthday, hell, I'll marry you."

She turned to look at him, her eyes wide. "Do you mean it?"

"Damn straight." He pecked a kiss on her cheek, then scooted back against the trailer, dipping the brim of his hat low over his eyes again. "Of course, by the time you turn thirty, you'll probably be married and have a litter of snot-nosed kids hanging onto your belt loops."

Or at least he hoped she did. Forrest Cunningham was a man whose word was as good as law...but he sure as hell wasn't planning on getting married. Even the thought of marriage and spending the rest of his life saddled with one woman made him shudder in revulsion.

One

Royal, Texas 1999

West Texas.

Damn if it wasn't the prettiest sight in the whole universe. And Forrest Cunningham should know. Over the years, his travels in the military and those as head of his family's cattle empire had provided him with the opportunity to see a good portion of the world.

But considering how, at the moment, his view of West Texas was limited to the interior of the Royal Diner with its smoke-stained walls, cracked vinyl-topped bar stools, chipped Formica-topped tables and a beat-up jukebox that had been sitting in the same spot since the Fifties...well, even *thinking* West Texas was the prettiest sight in the world was probably grounds enough to commit a man.

But, then, Forrest was already questioning his sanity.

It had all started a little over two weeks ago while he and several other members of the exclusive Texas Cattleman's Club had been on a secret mission in Europe to rescue a princess and her young son.

He snorted at the reminder of the woman whose rescue seemed to be at the core of his current level of discontent. A princess for God's sake. He glanced in the direction of the counter where the woman in question worked.

Beautiful. That was the only word to describe Anna von Oberland. A mane of thick blond hair. Dark green eyes. A figure that would make any man stand up at attention. Hell, even with an apron tied around her waist she managed to look regal.

A princess.

He snorted again and gave his head a shake as he turned his gaze to the smudged window and the view of the Royal Diner's parking lot where the wind was thickening the air with sand. A princess in Royal, Texas. Who'd have ever thought? But she was there. And she *was* a princess. Forrest could attest to both because he'd played a part in snatching her away from the squirrely prince who had wanted to force her into a marriage after her sister's tragic death so that he could gain control of her estate and merge their kingdoms.

The rescue mission—code-named Alpha—had been the brainchild of Gregory Hunt. Gregory's brother Blake and Sterling Churchill had made up the rest of the team. Hank Langley had footed the bill for the mission, though Forrest knew damn good and well Hank would have preferred to have been in on the action, rather than staying home and overseeing the operation from the comfort and safety of his office above the Texas Cattleman's Club.

The thought of his old friend and owner of the private men's club plowed a deeper row of discontent on Forrest's brow. Hank Langley was one of his oldest friends and the most eligible bachelor in Royal…or at least he had been. Now Hank was a married man.

And Sterling, too. Who would have ever thought Sterling would walk down that long aisle again? Not after his first marriage had gone sour on him. But he had. And now he had a wife, same as Hank, and seemed as happy as a dog with a new bone. And he was going to be a daddy before long.

Sterling a daddy…

Forrest felt the sense of desolation digging its way deeper inside of him and tried to rope it in before he sunk into a blue funk so deep he couldn't crawl out. Hell, he told himself, he had just turned thirty-five, was in the prime of his life, had more money than he could shake a stick at, and was the owner of the biggest ranch in West Texas. What did he have to feel blue about?

His shoulders slumped in despair. He didn't need a psychologist to figure out the answer to that question. He'd already spent hours cogitating on the problem himself and he'd finally come up with the answer.

He needed a wife.

And children.

What was the use of having an empire if a man didn't have somebody to pass it on to? Someone to carry on the Cunningham name?

The problem was there wasn't a woman in the entire county whom he wanted to marry. He'd already made a list of all the eligible females he knew, and one-by-one had crossed through their names, ruling them out as possible candidates for the position of the future Mrs. Forrest Cunningham.

"Would you like more coffee?"

Forrest whipped his head around to find Anna standing

beside his booth. She held up the coffeepot in silent invitation, its chipped and scarred handle a startling contrast to the graceful and delicate fingers curled around it. He wondered, not for the first time, if the Royal Diner was the best place to try to hide a royal princess. Anna von Oberland—dubbed Annie Grace by the members of the Alpha team in an effort to hide her true identity—stuck out like a rose in a patch of grease wood. He reared back, giving her room, and gestured toward his cup. "Yeah, you can warm it up for me."

She leaned over to pour and Forrest noticed that her hand shook a bit. Before he could dodge the hot steaming brew that sloshed over the cup's rim, it splattered across his lap, soaking quickly through his jeans and scalding his flesh.

Seeing what she'd done, Anna cried, "Oh, no!" and whipped a dish towel from the waistband of her apron and began dabbing frantically at the stain. Forrest sucked in a raw breath as her fingers moved dangerously close to his privates. He quickly closed his hand over hers.

"Keep that up and you're liable to warm up more than just my coffee."

She snapped her gaze to his. Her eyes grew wide and her mouth formed a perfect O as his meaning slowly registered. Quickly she snatched her hand from his and fisted it behind her back. "I'm sorry," she murmured, dropping her gaze in embarrassment.

Damn, but she was pretty, Forrest thought as he watched her cheeks turn an engaging shade of pink. Maybe... He quickly squelched the idea. Though nothing had been said, he was sure that there was still something between Anna and his buddy Greg Hunt. After all, it was Greg who Anna had contacted for help, and it was Greg who had headed up the mission to rescue her. And Forrest

Cunningham wasn't the kind of man to trespass on another man's territory.

He shot her a grin, hoping to put her at ease as he reached for a napkin to finish the job she'd started. "No damage done."

She gave a cautious look around, then eased closer. "Forrest? I was wondering…have you heard anything from Blake?"

The worry in her voice was obvious and explained the trembling in her hands. He supposed he'd be worried, too, if he was in her shoes. Blake was the last leg of the Alpha mission, and the one assigned to deliver Anna's niece and nephew to her in Royal.

A bachelor traveling halfway around the world with two babies in tow.

Forrest bit back a grin. He'd give anything to be a fly on the wall right now, so he could see Blake Hunt in the role of a nanny. Changing diapers, singing lullabies. Somehow the picture just didn't fit. But if anybody could do it, Blake could, he reminded himself. Blake was nothing if he wasn't resourceful.

Forrest gave Anna an encouraging smile. "Don't you worry that pretty little head of yours about Blake. He'll get 'em here safely. You'll see."

"It isn't that I don't trust him," she said uneasily. She caught her lower lip between her teeth again. "It's just that…well, being a single man, I doubt he knows very much about caring for infants."

Forrest shot her a wink. "That's what you think. Before he left on the mission, Blake spent days at the library reading every book they had on the subject. He even interviewed ladies around town on how to properly care for an infant. Created quite a stir with his questions, too," he added, chuckling.

Anna inhaled deeply, then managed a smile. "I'm sure you're right." She leaned to give his hand a grateful pat. "Thank you, Forrest. For everything," she added in a whisper, before turning away.

Forrest watched her cross back to the bar, his eyes going unerringly to the seductive sway of her hips. He gave his head a shake and forced his gaze back to the window. Don't even think it, he warned himself. Even if he didn't suspect that Greg had a prior claim on the princess, he knew that Anna wasn't the woman for him.

So who is? he asked himself, his frustration returning with a force stronger than the wind outside that was currently sandblasting his truck in the diner's parking lot. He'd already ruled out every eligible woman within a three hundred mile radius of Royal. There wasn't a single woman left with whom he'd want to share his name, much less his life.

Frowning, he glanced at his wristwatch and saw that it was almost two. He had promised to meet Becky at two-thirty and inspect a mare that he was having delivered to her ranch.

He started to rise, then slowly sank back down in the booth, his eyes going wide. "Rebecca Lee Sullivan," he whispered under his breath. Why hadn't he thought of Becky before now?

Becky as his wife. He toyed with the idea for a moment, weighing the possibilities. She'd lived next door to him for as long as he could remember and was as good a friend as a man could ask for. She liked ranching and horses and wasn't afraid to get her hands dirty, unlike most of the women he knew. She wasn't hard to look at, was self-reliant, and could rope and ride as well as any man, himself included.

Hell! Becky was the perfect woman for a rancher like him!

He quickly fished money from his pocket, tossed it on the table and grabbed his hat. As he strode for the door of the diner, he recalled a conversation that he and Becky had had years before, and a promise he'd made to her at the time.

If you're not married by your thirtieth birthday, hell, I'll marry you.

The good news was that Becky *hadn't* married and, if memory served him right, her thirtieth birthday was in November, less than six weeks away.

It was all he could do to keep from kicking up his heels as he headed for his truck. If he had his way—and Forrest usually did—he and Miss Rebecca Lee Sullivan would be married by the time her birthday rolled around.

It was all just a matter of him popping the question.

Forrest parked his truck about fifty feet from the round pen where Becky was working a colt and settled back to watch. The colt was one of Forrest's, bred and raised on the Cunningham ranch, the Golden Steer. He'd hauled the horse over to the Rusty Corral, Becky's family's place, just before leaving on the mission to Europe so that Becky could begin training him while he was gone. By the look of things, she'd made good use of the time. The colt was trotting smoothly along the wall of the pen, moving in and out of the obstacle course Becky had set up, while Becky turned a tight circle in the middle, her attention fixed on the young horse. Her arms were outstretched, forming a widemouthed V, one hand gripping a longe line clipped to the colt's halter and the other dragging a whip along the ground aimed at the colt's rear hooves.

Forrest pursed his lips thoughtfully and watched, his

gaze focused not on the colt, but on the woman. He assessed her as he would a brood mare he was thinking of buying, or a registered cow he was thinking of adding to his herd—one eye narrowed, his brow furrowed in concentration, while he studied her conformation.

Though she was skinny as a rail, she was built tough; Forrest knew that for a fact. And tough was important when a man was thinking of taking on a wife who would be required to live on a ranch as big and isolated as the Golden Steer. He moved his gaze on a slow journey from her battered, sweat-stained hat, down her spine and settled it on the seat of her faded jeans. A frayed tear just below one cheek of her butt exposed a strip of olive-toned skin.

When he realized that he was staring and what he was staring at, he forced his gaze back up to her hips. They were a little narrow, he acknowledged with a frown, trying not to think about that strip of bare skin, but seemed wide enough to handle a birth without much trouble. And though her breasts were small, he didn't figure size counted much when it came to nursing a babe...and Cunningham women always nursed their young. The natural way, Forrest's dad had always insisted, whether discussing animals or humans, was the only way. Like his father, Forrest believed that nature knew best and lived by her rules.

She'll do, he told himself confidently and shouldered open the door of his truck. Standing, he paused a moment to stretch out the kinks in his legs, then slammed the door and headed for the round pen. Becky glanced up at the sound.

A smile bloomed on her face when she saw him. "Hey, Woody!" she called, shoving her hat farther back on her head.

"Hey, yourself," he returned, not even wincing at the

nickname she'd assigned to him years before. He propped a custom-made boot on the corral's lowest rail, his forearms along the rail at shoulder level, and gave her a nod of approval. "He's lookin' good."

"Better than good," she corrected. "Watch this." Taking a firmer grip on the longe line, she gave the whip a snap in the air and ordered, "Lope." The colt stepped easily into the faster gait, his head high, his tail streaming behind him. Becky turned slowly in the center of the ring, her gaze fixed on the animal as he circled the pen, weaving a path around the barriers she'd set up, and pushing his way through a tarp she'd strung between two poles. "Whoa!" she called suddenly and followed the command with a slight tug on the line. The colt sank bank on his haunches, churning dust as he slid to a stop.

Pleased with the demonstration, Becky moved to the colt's head and rubbed the white star that ran from his forehead to his nose. "Good, boy," she murmured, pressing her cheek against his. "Good, boy." He turned his head slightly and gave her a playful nudge. She laughed as she coiled the longe line in her gloved hand, then led the colt to where Forrest stood. "Better than good, right?"

Though he knew she was looking for praise, Forrest couldn't resist teasing her a little. "Depends on a person's definition of good."

Becky shot him a sour look, then turned to tie the colt at the rail. "How many green horses have you seen that wouldn't have spooked at that flapping tarp?"

"A few."

Her scowl deepened and she gave her slip knot a yank, testing it, before she headed for the gate. Forrest opened it for her and waited while she stepped through.

"Ingrate," she muttered darkly as she passed by him.

"Show-off," he returned, grinning, then locked the gate behind her.

"Where've you've been keeping yourself?" she said irritably. "I haven't laid eyes on you since before you took off on that vacation in Europe you were so hush-hush about."

Though he knew exactly where he'd been—wining and dining the female population of Ward County while ruling out all the possibilities as candidates for the position as his future wife—Forrest thought it best not to tell Becky that. She was a woman, after all, and might not like the idea that she wasn't his first choice. "Oh, around," he said vaguely.

She snorted and pulled off her hat. "When are they delivering the mare?"

"Anytime now," he replied, watching as her red hair settled around her shoulders. He'd never noticed how thick her long hair was, or the golden highlights hidden in it, until that moment when the sun hit the red mane, panning the gold from its depths. But then he'd never really thought much about the feminine side of Becky. To him, she was a buddy, same as Sterling and Hank.

While he watched, fascinated by this new side of her he was discovering, she bent at the waist and scrubbed her fingers through her hair, separating the damp locks, then straightened, flipping her hair back over her head and behind her shoulders. The sun caught the red and gold highlights and turned them to fire.

Redheaded kids. Forrest pondered the idea for a moment, wondering if Becky's red gene would dominate his black one…then decided a redhead might be a welcome change among the traditionally black-headed Cunninghams.

Yep, Rebecca Lee Sullivan would do just fine as the

future Mrs. Forrest Cunningham. Trying to think of a way to pop the question to her, he draped an arm along her shoulders and guided her toward the barn and the only strip of shade in sight. "Did you miss me while I was gone?"

"'Bout as much as I'd miss a toothache."

He bumped his hip against hers. "*Aww,* come on now, Becky. You know you missed me."

She stopped once they reached the shade and folded her arms over her breasts as she turned to look up at him. "Did you miss me?" she returned pointedly.

"As a matter of fact, I did."

Her brows shot up at his unexpected response, then down into a frown. "Yeah, right," she muttered and slapped her hat against her thigh to shake the dust from it. She turned her back to the barn and propped a worn boot heel against its side as she settled her shoulders against the weathered wood.

"No, I really did," he insisted. "In fact, I was thinking about you just this afternoon while I was eating lunch at the Royal Diner."

She glanced up at him. "Why?" she asked dryly. "Did you have indigestion, or something?"

Forrest laughed and reached over to tousle her hair. "Naw. I was just thinking about you—us. You know," he said, suddenly feeling awkward, "how long we've known each other, and all."

She peered at him closely. "You didn't get hit in the head, or anything, while you were in Europe, did you?"

Forrest snorted and pulled off his hat, slowly turning it by its brim as he studied it. "No. There's nothing wrong with my head."

Becky gave her chin a quick jerk of approval. "Good. You had me worried there for a minute."

Forrest moved to stand beside her, mirroring her posture—boot heel and shoulders braced against the barn wall. He stared out across Sullivan land to the fence that marked the border of the Golden Steer. "How long have you and your dad lived here?" he asked. He was close enough to feel her shoulder move when she lifted it in a shrug.

"I don't know. 'Bout twenty years or so, I'd guess."

"Twenty years," he repeated, then shook his head. "That's a long time. A mighty long time."

Becky gave him a curious look. "Yeah, I suppose."

"You have a birthday coming up, don't you?"

"Yeah," she replied slowly, then scrunched up her nose and leaned to look more closely at him. "Are you *sure* you didn't get hit in the head?"

Frustrated, Forrest pushed himself away from the wall, and whirled to face her. He'd forgotten how aggravating Becky could be at times. "Why do you keep asking me if there's something wrong with my head?"

She lifted a shoulder again, then slid down the wall until she was sitting on the ground. Dropping her hat over her upraised knees, she brushed dust from its crown. "I don't know," she mumbled. "I guess it's because you're not usually this sentimental."

He hauled in a deep breath, forcing himself to calm down. He couldn't very well propose marriage while they were arguing. "No, I'm not. But that doesn't mean I don't think about things now and again." He hunkered down in front of her. "Do you remember the time we were out rounding up steers? You would've been eighteen or so at the time, and you were crying because no one had invited you to the Cattleman's Ball."

Her lips thinned at the reminder and she looked up at him, her green eyes sparking fire. "I don't cry," she informed him coldly. "And I don't give a hoot about going to any old ball. Never have."

Forrest had to count backward from ten to keep from debating the issue with her. He knew damn good and well she'd cried. He remembered the day well, because he'd never seen her cry before…and not once, since. "Yeah, well, anyway, you said something that day—or rather asked me something—that I've never forgotten. You said to me, 'Woody, do you think I'll ever get married?'" He gave his head a rueful shake as he turned his gaze to his hat. "Damn near broke my heart." He cocked his head to look at her. "I promised you right then and there that if you weren't married by your thirtieth birthday, that I'd marry you myself."

He watched her eyes grow as big as half-dollars and her throat convulse as if she was having trouble swallowing. Her lips moved a couple of times, but no sound emerged. Finally she managed to get out, "W-why are you telling me all this?"

Forrest pushed himself to his feet and looked down at her as he settled his hat back on his head. "Well, Becky," he said, swelling his chest a bit and giving the waist of his jeans a confident hitch, "it's because you're gonna be thirty soon and destined to spinsterhood. I think it's high time I made good on my promise."

She was up and off the ground so fast that Forrest wasn't sure she'd ever been sitting. Then her finger was stabbing into his chest and he was backing up and she was pressing forward, her eyes narrowed to slits and her mouth thinned to one white line of fury. "Marry you!" she all but screamed at him. "You egotistical, thickheaded mule. I wouldn't marry you if you were the last man on earth!" She gave him a shove that sent him stumbling backward. Another shove and his boot heel hooked on a rock and he went sprawling, arms flailing. He landed flat on his back, knocking the breath from him and making him see stars. When his vision cleared, Becky was leaning over him, her face as red as her hair. "A spinster, huh? Well, let me tell you something, buster. I'd rather—"

Forrest had heard enough. He caught her ankle and gave it a tug, jerking her off her feet. She landed in the middle of his chest with a thud and a muffled *whoomph*. Before she could catch her breath, he locked both arms around her back, holding her against him. They were chest to chest, their noses inches apart. "Now, you listen to me, Rebecca Lee Sullivan," he warned. "I'm offering you marriage, the opportunity to be my wife. There are women all over Wade County who would give their eyeteeth for a chance to become Mrs. Forrest Cunningham."

"Who?" she demanded angrily. "Name one."

The question caught Forrest off guard, and it took him a minute to come up with a name. "Fanny Lou Farmer," he blurted out.

Becky snorted her opinion of Forrest's choice. "That pie-faced bimbo?"

"And there's Marylee Porter." Warming to the challenge, he added, "*And* Pansy Estrich." He knew how much Becky hated the phony, silicone-inflated blonde.

Becky squirmed, trying to break free of his hold. "If you're even considering marrying a one of them, it just proves that your brains are located somewhere south of your belt buckle."

Though he was sure she'd meant to insult him, the accusation drew a smile. "What's wrong, Becky? Jealous?"

She immediately stilled, then shot him a look that would melt creosote off a fence post. "As if a one of those women has anything that I'd be jealous of." She humphed, then gave his chest a frustrated shove. "Let me up."

"Not until you say you'll marry me."

She stilled again, her gaze going to his. Something he saw there—was it fear? Hope? Whatever it was, it scared the hell out of him...but not nearly as much as her next words.

"Why, Woody?" she asked, her voice a raw whisper. "Why do you want to marry me?"

It was Forrest's turn to squirm. The truth was that he was in desperate need of a wife, but he wasn't a man who liked to expose his vulnerabilities. A shrewd negotiator from the top of his Stetson to the tips of his custom-made boots, when working a deal, whether in oil leases or cattle futures, he made it a rule to never reveal his weaknesses. "Because I promised I would," he said instead. "Besides," he added irritably, "it's not as if men are knocking down your door with offers."

Angrily Becky twisted free of him and jumped to her feet. She planted her fists on her hips as she glared down at him. "Well, I won't marry you."

Slowly Forrest sat up, locking his arms around his knees as he returned her angry look. "Give me one good reason."

"I...I—I've already got a fiancé." She immediately stooped to scoop her hat from the ground and, in doing so, managed to hide her face from him.

"You're lying."

She popped up faster than a jack-in-the-box. "Are you calling me a liar?"

"Damn straight. If you had a boyfriend, I'd know it."

She made a production of dusting off her hat...and avoiding his gaze. "You don't know *everything* about me," she mumbled.

"Well, you sure as hell didn't have a boyfriend when I left town!"

"This was—well, it was rather sudden."

Forrest braced a hand on the ground and levered himself to his feet, then stooped to retrieve his own hat. "Sudden, hell. I'd call it a damn miracle."

She shot him a dark look, which he ignored.

"So who is this mysterious fiancé of yours? Anybody I know?"

She headed for the barn, her chin tipped high enough to catch water. "I doubt it."

Forrest followed close on her heels. "Well, who is he, then?"

"He's just a guy I met."

"Where?"

Her steps slowed for a moment, then sped right back up as if she was trying to outrun him and his questions. "At a...at a cattle auction."

"Is he from around here?"

She stopped in front of a stall and unlatched the gate. "No. He's from—Wichita."

"Kansas?"

"Yeah," she agreed a little too quickly, and ducked inside the stall, "Kansas."

His eyes narrowed in suspicion, Forrest watched her as she checked the level of water in the bucket. "So how long have y'all been engaged?"

"A week."

"When's the wedding?"

"Oh, I don't know," she replied vaguely. "We haven't set a date."

"What's his name?"

She whirled to look at him, her eyes wide and unblinking. "His name?" she repeated dully.

The look on her face was the same one she'd worn the time Forrest's mother had cornered the two of them, furious because someone had eaten the pecan pie she'd baked for the church social that evening. She'd been sure that he and Becky had eaten it. Though Forrest had spun a convincing tale in an attempt to escape a sure whipping, when his mother had turned to Becky to verify his story, her guilty look had given them both away.

"Yeah," he muttered, watching her carefully, "his name. You know, how he signs his checks."

"Oh. His name's…John. John Smith."

Forrest pursed his lips as she stepped from the stall. Yep, she was lying. He was sure of it. Becky never had been any good at maintaining a poker face. And John Smith. Even the name sounded made-up. "Sure it isn't Doe?" he goaded. "As in John Doe?"

She glanced at him, frowning, then scooped feed from the bin into a bucket. "No. It's Smith. With a *y* instead of an *i*." Then, as if as an afterthought, she added, "And with an *e* at the end."

"John Smythe." Forrest tossed back his head and laughed. Smythe with a *y* instead of an *i* and an *e* tacked on at the end. That's prime, Becky. Really prime."

She stormed past him and back into the stall, refusing to look at him. "You got a problem with my fiancé's name?" she snapped.

"No." He stepped back as she dumped the oats into the stall's bin, dodging the dust that shot into the air. "But I think you're making all this up."

She caught the bucket's handle in one hand, and smiled sweetly at him. "What's the matter, Woody? You jealous?"

He reared back, amazed that she would suggest such a thing.

"Hell, no!"

Her smile turned smug. "Yes, you are." She swung the empty bucket at her side as she retraced her steps to the feed bin. "Your male ego is showing. You don't want to believe that I might actually *prefer* marrying someone other than you."

Before Forrest could form a response, a horn honked outside.

Becky glanced up, then quickly dropped the bucket back into the feed bin when a truck pulled past the door. "There's your mare," she said, heading for the opening.

Frustrated by the interruption, Forrest trailed her. "We aren't through with this discussion, yet," he warned.

"You may not be, but I am," she returned, then yelled, "Hey, Slick! Whatcha got in there?"

Slick Richards slid from behind the wheel of his dually, grinning. "The prettiest little mare this side of heaven."

Becky clapped a hand on Slick's back as she walked with him to the rear of the trailer. "Heck, Slick, that's what you say every time you deliver a horse over here."

Slick gave his chin a jerk in Forrest's direction by way of greeting as he swung open the rear doors. "Have I ever lied?"

Laughing, Becky hopped up inside the trailer while the two men waited outside. When she got her first look at the mare, she whistled low under her breath. "Ho-le-e-ey smoke." She took a cautious step deeper into the trailer's shadowed interior. "How far along is she?"

"She'll be dropping her foal within the next two or three weeks."

Becky laid a hand on the mare's swollen side, then smoothed it over her shoulder and up along her neck. "She's a beaut, Slick. A real beaut." She untied the lead rope and gently backed the mare from the trailer, clucking softly. The horse balked a bit when she reached the rear door and her hoof hit nothing but air. "Easy, mama," Becky soothed. "You're doing just fine."

Forrest stepped back, giving them room, then moved to Becky's side once she and the mare had safely reached the ground. "She give you any trouble?" he asked Slick as he took the lead rope from Becky's hand.

"Sweetest little lady I've ever had the privilege to haul," he replied.

Forrest smiled when the mare snuffled his hand, looking for a treat. He rubbed a palm up her face to scratch her between the ears, his smile growing. "She's a sweetheart, all right." He angled his head toward Becky and his smile slipped down into a scowl. "Unlike some females I know."

Becky wasn't crying. She never cried. She just had something in her eye was all. She sniffed and dragged her wrist across her cheek, swiping at the telltale moisture, before reaching to remove the mare's halter. Once free, the horse turned immediately to the trough and the waiting feed. Becky watched her for a moment, her thoughts on the marriage proposal Woody had offered.

…because you're gonna be thirty soon and destined to spinsterhood. I think it's high time I made good on my promise.

She slapped the halter against the side of her leg. "Darn your sorry hide, Forrest Cunningham," she swore and stomped from the stall. When she turned to lock the gate behind her, her efforts were handicapped by the hot angry tears that blinded her.

She'd waited for years to hear a marriage proposal from Woody…but not one like that. A spinster! She dashed a hand at the tears again, then hooked the halter over a nail on the barn wall. "Like I'm some kind of charity case, or something," she muttered disagreeably. She sniffed, fighting the sting of the insult, the hurt…but finally sank onto a bale of hay, wrapped her arms around her waist, bent double and gave in to the tears. She sobbed until her head ached and her eyes swelled almost shut. She cried until there were no more tears left to cry.

When she was sure the well had run dry, she gave her face a brisk scrub, sucked in a deep, shuddering breath and told herself to buck up. There were worse things in life than being called a spinster and having a marriage proposal offered out of pity. She wasn't sure what those things were, but, given the time, she was sure she could come up with one or two.

After all, she reminded herself, it wasn't as if she'd ever really believed that Woody would propose to her. If nothing else, she was a realist. She knew she was no raving beauty, that she didn't have the social graces required to mingle with the folks Woody ran with.

But the heck of it was, he *had* asked her…and had hurt her feelings in the process. Granted, she was no debutante, but didn't she deserve romance as much as any other woman? Was it too much to ask to have an "I love you" thrown in there somewhere?

…*say you'll marry me.*

A sigh shuddered through her.

She'd dreamed of hearing Woody say those words to her for more years than she could remember. From the time she was thirteen and had first become aware of him as more than just the boy next door, she'd wished on the first star she'd seen every night that he would fall in love with her. *Starlight, star bright, first star I see tonight, I wish I may, I wish I might have the wish I wish tonight.* She'd even hoped to double her chances by wishing on every load of hay she'd ever seen. *Load of hay, load of hay, make a wish and look away.* And she'd never once looked back at the load of hay, after making her wish, for fear her wish wouldn't come true if she did.

And now she'd blown it. Just because Woody hadn't proposed to her with the pretty words that she'd imagined he'd use, she'd turned him down flat.

No, she corrected miserably, dropping her elbows onto her knees and her face onto her palms. She hadn't just turned him down. She'd lied to him.

She groaned, raking her fingers through her hair. What on earth had possessed her to concoct that wild tale about having a fiancé? She didn't have a fiancé. Heck! She'd never even had a regular boyfriend!

Pride, she told herself. That was her problem and always had been. Woody often teased her, saying that when God was passing out pride, she must have thought He'd said pie and asked for a double helping.

She chuckled at the memory, then felt another swell of tears bubble up in her throat. Oh, Lord, what was she going to do? she cried silently. If only she could roll back the clock, she'd bury her pride so deep it couldn't find her, and say yes to Woody's proposal, even if he had offered it out of pity.

But she couldn't roll back the clock, she reminded herself. And even if she could, she knew she'd react the same darn way, because she really didn't want to marry Woody if he didn't love her. She wanted his love as much as she wanted him.

A horse nickered and with a sigh, Becky pushed herself to her feet, reminded of the chores that waited. While she fed the stock, she told herself that spinsterhood really wasn't all that bad. After all, she didn't have a man underfoot all the time, expecting her to cook his dinner or wash his dirty clothes, as other women did. And there was nobody to demand her attention or her time. She could do what she wanted and when she wanted to do it.

The truth was, Rebecca Lee Sullivan was alone.

But, then, she always had been.

Two

"Hank, I need a wife."

"Sorry, I'm already taken."

"Funny," Forrest mumbled, scowling.

Hank reared back in his chair, hooking the heels of his custom-made boots on the chair's lowest rung, then took a quick look around to make sure Henry, the maître d' of the Texas Cattleman's Club, wasn't around. Owner, or not, even Hank Langley wasn't allowed to abuse the club's furniture. "Wasn't trying to be funny. Just stating a fact."

Sterling Churchill laughed, but quickly swallowed his amusement when Forrest directed the scowl his way. Sterling leaned to peer closely at his friend. "You're serious about this wife business, aren't you?"

Forrest picked up his beer. "Yeah, I am." He took a long swallow, then set the frosted mug down with a frustrated sigh. "The hell of it is, there aren't any single women left in the whole dad-blamed county."

"Pansy's still available," Hank offered and won another frown from Forrest. "Just trying to be helpful," he said, and gave Sterling a conspiratorial wink.

Catching Hank's drift and ready to help him give their friend a hard time, Sterling suggested, "There's always Martha Jo. I believe she's between husbands right now."

Forrest rolled his eyes. "I want a wife, not a damn bottle blond looking for another alimony check."

Sterling pursed his lips thoughtfully. "Well, I suppose if you're that picky you could put an ad in the Midland paper. Folks are doing that more and more these days." He drew a line in the air with his finger. "It could read something like this... 'Wife wanted. No bottle blonds need apply.'"

"Yeah," Hank tossed in, "and you could add 'no prior experience required' which might cut down on the number of divorcees who respond."

Forrest fell back against his chair in disgust. "You boys ought to take this show on the road."

"Now, Forrest," Hank soothed, trying to hide a grin. "We were only funnin' with you."

"Well, I'm not laughing. I need a wife, dammit." He leaned forward, bracing his arms on the table and curling his hands around his mug. He stared at his beer a moment, then cocked his head and narrowed an eye at Sterling. "Has Becky said anything to you about getting married?"

"Becky? Becky Sullivan?"

"How many Becky's do you know?"

Sterling shrugged. "Just the one."

"Well, has she?"

"No." Sterling grinned sheepishly. "But then I didn't say anything to her before I got married, either." He shook his head slowly as he absorbed what Forrest had just revealed. "Becky getting married. I'll just be damned."

"I didn't say she *was* getting married. I simply asked you if she'd said anything to you about it."

"Well, hell, Forrest," Sterling complained. "Is she getting married, or not?"

Forrest frowned. "I don't know, but earlier this afternoon, she told me she had a fiancé. Personally I think she was lying."

"Why would she lie about a thing like that?"

His gaze on his beer mug, Forrest turned the glass slowly between his hands. "Probably because she was mad at me."

A longtime friend of Becky's, Sterling leaned forward in his chair, ready to defend her if necessary. "What did you do to her?"

"I asked her to marry me."

Sterling's eyebrows shot up. "The hell you say!"

"Damn sure did, but she refused me. Said she was already engaged. Of course, she told me that *after* she knocked me down."

Hank held up a hand. "Whoa, hold on a minute. Let me get this straight. You asked Becky to marry you, and she knocked you down?"

"Well, she didn't exactly knock me down. She shoved me and my boot heel hooked on a rock and I fell down."

"Why'd she shove you?"

"How the hell would I know? She's a woman, isn't she? Women do crazy things all the time."

Sterling and Hank shared a knowing look, both men aware of their friend's lack of finesse with women. Though never short on female companionship, Forrest had never learned the finer points in courting a woman. Probably because he'd never had to. Women just naturally flocked to him, without him having to put forth much effort.

"Maybe you better tell us how you worded this proposal," Sterling suggested.

"All I did was remind her of a promise that I made to her years ago about marrying her myself if she hadn't hooked up with somebody by the time she turned thirty. Since her thirtieth birthday is less than six weeks away, I told her that I was ready to make good on my promise."

Having already heard about this pact from Becky just a few weeks before, Sterling asked, "Is that all?"

Forrest furrowed his brow, trying to remember the exact conversation. "No, I believe I mentioned something about saving her from spinsterhood."

Hank let his head fall back. "Oh, Lord," he groaned.

"And what was wrong with my proposal?" Forrest wanted to know.

"Hell, Forrest, you insulted her," Hank told him. "No woman likes to be referred to as a spinster." He sighed heavily. "Sterling, looks like you and me are gonna have to give Forrest here some lessons on how to properly court a woman."

Forrest's chest swelled in indignation. "Just because the two of you have each walked the aisle twice, doesn't make y'all experts on the subject."

"We have wives, don't we? And *you* don't," Sterling reminded him.

Forrest waved a hand in dismissal. "Forget it. Becky's already engaged—or at least she *says* she is."

"Maybe she *is* getting married," Sterling said in his friend's defense. "Becky's not one to lie."

"She is this time," Forrest argued stubbornly, "and I intend to prove it."

Forrest didn't waste any time in trying to prove Becky was lying. As soon as he finished his beer, he left the Texas Cattleman's Club and headed straight for the Rusty Corral. As he drove over the cattle guard at the ranch's entrance, he noted the barbed-wire fence was sagging in a couple of places and made a mental note to send one of his men over to repair it.

He knew Becky would pitch a fit when she discovered what he'd done. He'd fought similar battles with her before when he'd meddled in her business. But he couldn't very well sit by and let her ranch fall down around her. God knew the poor woman was doing all she could to keep the place going.

He frowned as his thoughts shifted to Becky's daddy, Shorty Sullivan. The man ought to be horse-whipped and dragged across Ozark Salt Lake naked, letting the salt burn his raw wounds, he thought angrily. Leaving a woman alone to do a man's work. And the old goat had been doing it for years.

Forrest remembered the first time he'd discovered that Shorty had taken off and left his daughter alone on the ranch. Becky couldn't have been more than twelve or thirteen at the time. Forrest had called late one evening to ask her if she'd help out with a roundup, and, when no one had answered the phone, he'd decided to just drive over. He'd found her in the barn wrapped up in a blanket and huddled in a corner of her horse's stall. The poor kid had been scared to death...but wouldn't admit it. She was that stubborn.

And she hadn't changed much over the years. He couldn't count the times that he and his family had tried to help her out when times were hard. But she wouldn't accept their assistance, considered it charity. Forrest himself was the one who had finally come up with the idea of offering her the job of checking daily on the windmills that dotted the Golden Steer to make sure they were still pumping the water that was so vital for their herds.

A job Becky could accept. Charity she wouldn't.

The job had grown over the years to include Becky riding Golden Steer horses while she made the windmill circuit. When he'd offered her the first string of horses, he'd used the excuse that he needed her to keep the horses in shape for roundups and was willing to pay her for riding them. It wasn't long before he'd added the job of Becky training the horses, too. Thus, Becky had ended up on the Golden Steer payroll, and the Cunninghams had all slept easier, knowing that the girl wasn't going to starve to death right beneath their noses.

Forrest gave his head a rueful shake as he parked his truck in front of the barn on the Rusty Corral. Stubborn. That's what Becky Lee Sullivan was. And her saying that she couldn't marry him because she was already engaged was just another example of that stubbornness.

Anxious to pump her for information on this fantasy fiancé of hers, he climbed from his truck and headed for the barn, suspecting he'd find Becky inside with the new mare. Sure enough, he found her in the stall, talking softly to the horse while she brushed her down.

"How's she doing?"

Startled, Becky jumped at the sound of his voice, then, with a huff, went back to her grooming. "Fine. Doesn't seem to have suffered any ill effects from the trip."

Forrest opened the stall door and stepped inside. "Good." He ran a hand along the horse's neck, letting the mare know he was there, then rested his arm along the animal's spine as he watched Becky brush tangles from the horse's tail. "Spoiling her already," he teased.

"She likes the attention."

By the defensive tone in her voice, he knew she was still angry with him and was spoiling for a fight. But Forrest didn't want to argue with her. He wanted the truth and was determined to get it.

"I'm sure she does," he replied placidly. He gave the horse's rump a pat then moved to the side of the stall and leaned his back against it to watch Becky work.

"Saw Sterling earlier," he offered conversationally.

She grunted an acknowledgment, but didn't respond.

"He seemed surprised to hear that you were engaged."

Her hand froze for a split second, then she tossed down the brush, trading it for a metal comb. "And they say women gossip," she muttered.

Forrest bit back a grin. "I wasn't gossiping. Just shootin' the breeze with friends over a beer at the Cattleman's Club."

"Gossiping," she repeated firmly.

Forrest lifted a shoulder. "I figured you'd have told him about this fiancé of yours, being as y'all are such good friends, and all."

She gave the comb a hard tug, yanking at a stubborn tangle. "Didn't see that it was all that important," she mumbled.

Forrest widened his eyes, feigning shock. "Why, Becky Lee, I'm surprised at you. Marriage is one of the most important steps a person takes in life."

She grunted again and tossed aside the comb. Turning her back to him, she bent over and lifted the mare's rear leg to inspect her hoof. "Make yourself useful and hand me that pick."

Her position offered Forrest a perfect view of her backside. In all the years he'd known Becky, he'd never once given her figure a second thought...but he did now. Heart-shaped, the cheeks of her butt filled out the denim jeans nicely. Without meaning to, he found himself lowering his gaze and looking for the tear he'd noticed earlier and that strip of exposed flesh.

Unfortunately she'd showered and changed since he'd last seen her and had put on a clean pair of jeans. This pair sported no tears or frays, no peeks at what lay beneath.

Disappointed, he plucked the hoof pick from the tack box and moved to hand it to her. "Getting married is serious business," he said, watching her closely. "I certainly hope that you aren't rushing into anything."

Setting her jaw, she strained as she worked a clump of caked mud and stones from the horse's hoof. "I'm not rushing into anything. Like I said, we haven't set a date yet."

"A long engagement, huh?" He nodded his approval. "That's probably wise. Too many people rush into marriage without giving themselves a chance to really get to know each other first."

She lowered the horse's leg and straightened, then slowly turned to face him. "And I suppose you consider yourself an expert on the subject of marriage?"

"I never claimed to be an expert."

"Then why are you offering *me* advice?"

Forrest took a steadying breath. He wouldn't argue with her, he told himself. Once they got started, they'd wind up in a spitting contest for sure. They usually did. Instead he took the hoof pick from her and dropped it back in the tack box. Draping an arm around her shoulders, he guided her from the stall. "Because I'm your friend, and friends worry about each other."

"I don't need you worrying about me. I can take care of myself."

In the alleyway, he placed both hands on her shoulders

and turned her around to face him. Bending his knees a little, he looked directly into her eyes. "I know that, Becky. Your independence is one of the things that I admire most about you." He gave her shoulders a reassuring squeeze. "But I'd feel a whole lot better if I knew something about this fiancé of yours. In fact," he said, and tucked her beneath his arm, aiming her for the barn doors and the outside, "I'd like to run a trace on him. You know, find out a little about his past. Hank's got a few contacts that I can take advantage of."

She stopped so fast, dust churned beneath her boots. "Run a trace on him!"

"Well, yeah," he said, trying his best to look innocent. "Just to make sure that he's on the up-and-up. All I need is his full name, his address. If you have his social security number or his driver's license number, though, it would help."

He watched her face redden, her lips tremble, and was sure that she was near breaking point. Any second now she would admit that she didn't really have a fiancé, that she'd made the whole thing up. Then Forrest could pop the question again, offering to marry her himself. By November he'd have himself a wife.

A second ticked by, then two, and Becky's face turned redder and redder until it was as bright red as her hair. Too late Forrest realized that it wasn't guilt that was turning her face colors. It was anger.

"Now, Becky," he said, backing up a cautious step.

"Don't you 'now, Becky' me," she warned, closing the distance right back up. "I don't need you or anybody else running my life for me. I've been taking care of myself for years, and doing a darn good job of it, I might add. So you can take your friendly offer to run a trace on my fiancé and get the heck off of my land, and stay off!"

Realizing that she had him retreating again, Forrest stopped and braced his hands on his hips. "Dang it, Becky! I'm not trying to run your life. I'm just trying to protect you."

"I don't need protecting."

"Maybe, maybe not," he shot back, then huffed a frustrated breath when her chin went up. "Aww, Beck," he said softening his tone, "I don't want to fight with you."

"Then what *do* you want?" she cried. "You come over here and insult me by suggesting that my fiancé is some sort of con man."

"I didn't say any such thing."

"You wanted to run a trace on him, didn't you?"

"Well, yeah, but that was just so I could...well, so I could find out a little more about him."

"You don't need to know anything about him. *I'm* the one who's marrying him, not you."

Hearing her claim she was getting married so emphatically did something to Forrest's ability to breathe. He was so sure that this engagement business had all been a lie. For the first time, he wondered if this fiancé of hers might really exist. "You're serious about marrying this guy, aren't you?"

She wheeled around, turning her back to him, and folded her arms across her breasts. "Yes, I am."

He stared at her back while his heart sunk lower and lower in his chest. He thought he'd been blue earlier, but that particular shade of blue didn't hold a candle to his current state of mind. Becky had always been in his life. His buddy. His friend. Hell, she'd been like a kid sister to him.

And now she was getting married.

Without a word of farewell, he turned and headed for his truck.

As soon as Forrest left, Becky hopped in her own rat-tletrap truck and headed straight for Miss Manie's, the one woman in town to whom she ran when she was troubled about something. It wasn't until she'd turned onto the woman's street, that she remembered that Miss Manie had married and was living in Midland now, which was an indication of just how distraught Becky was.

But as she passed by the house, she saw a light on in the kitchen. Hoping the light wasn't just a security mea-sure, she whipped her truck onto the driveway, hopped out and jogged to the porch. She rapped twice on the screen door, then rammed her hands deep into her pockets and rocked back on her boot heels, waiting.

The sound of voices drifted from the back of the house and Becky realized that Miss Manie wasn't alone, a pros-pect she hadn't considered before. Not wanting to discuss her troubles in front of Miss Manie's new husband, she was ready to turn tail and run when the porch light blinked on and the door opened. A young woman stepped into the opening.

"Well, hi...Becky, isn't it?" the woman asked uncer-tainly.

Becky yanked off her cowboy hat, and nodded. "Yes, ma'am. Becky Sullivan."

The woman smiled. "I thought so. I've heard quite a bit about you." She extended her hand. "I'm Callie Lang-ley, Hank's wife, and Miss Manie's niece."

Becky had heard about Hank's marriage, and had heard, too, that his wife was a good deal younger than he was. But nobody had mentioned how pretty she was, or how fragile-looking. Feeling clumsy and boyish in comparison, Becky shook the offered hand. "Pleased to meet you." She glanced behind Callie. "I saw the light and was hop-ing to catch Miss Manie at home."

Callie opened the door wider, gesturing for Becky to come inside. "She's here. We were just about to have a cup of tea. Why don't you join us?"

The idea of a tea party with the two women had Becky backing up. "Oh, I wouldn't want to disturb y'all or anything."

Callie caught Becky's hand before she could escape. "You aren't disturbing a thing, and I know that Aunt Manie will be glad to see you."

"Who's that at the door, Callie?"

Callie called over her shoulder, "Becky Sullivan, Aunt Manie."

Miss Manie appeared in the kitchen doorway. "Rebecca Lee Sullivan," she warned sternly, "you better hope your boots are clean."

Becky glanced down at her feet, then back up at Miss Manie and grinned. "Yes, ma'am. They're clean."

Manie turned back to her kitchen. "Better be. Last time you were here, you tracked manure on my freshly waxed floor."

Becky winced as she headed for the kitchen, dodging packing boxes stacked in the short hall. "Sorry 'bout that, Miss Manie."

"Sorry doesn't wax floors," Miss Manie replied sharply, but when she turned to look at Becky, the twinkle in her eyes took the sting out of her words. She waved her toward a chair. "Have a seat. Callie and I were just having us a cup of herbal tea."

Becky hooked her hat on the back of the chair, then sat down. She wrinkled her nose as Callie placed a fragile cup and saucer in front of her, then poured steaming tea into it. "What is it?" she asked suspiciously as she dipped her head to peer at the lightly colored brew.

"Chamomile leaves. Settles a person's nerves," Callie

explained, then added pointedly, "Looks as if yours could use some settling."

"That obvious, huh?"

Callie gave Becky's hand a reassuring pat before taking a seat beside her. "I may be a Langley now, but I was a Riley first, and we Rileys have the gift of intuition. Isn't that right, Aunt Manie?" she asked, turning to her aunt for confirmation.

"We do for a fact." Manie pushed a plate of spiced tea cookies toward Becky. "What brings you over here this time of night, Rebecca Lee?"

Becky waved away the offered cookies, sure that anything she put in her stomach would come right back up. She was feeling that sick over the lie she'd told Woody. "I need some advice, Miss Manie. You see…I…well, that is to say, I…"

"Well, spit it out, girl," Miss Manie snapped impatiently.

Becky shifted uncomfortably in her chair and cast a quick, self-conscious glance Callie's way before dropping her gaze to her cup. "It's kind of personal," she murmured.

"Oh, don't mind, Callie," Miss Manie said with a dismissive wave of her hand. "She worked in a doctor's office before moving to Texas and is accustomed to keeping things she hears under her bonnet."

After offering Callie an apologetic look, Becky fiddled with the handle of her teacup a moment before mumbling, "I—I told a lie."

Miss Manie snorted. "I'm sure it's not the first one you've told, nor will it be the last. So what makes this teewydie so special?"

Miss Manie had a way of getting to the heart of the matter that Becky had always respected, which was why she had often come to the older woman with her problems over the years. "I told the lie to Woody and now I don't know how to go about telling him the truth."

"Woody is Forrest Cunningham," Manie explained for Callie's benefit, then turned back to Becky. "What'd you tell him?"

"I told him I had a fiancé."

Miss Manie reared back and looked at Becky askance. "A fiancé?"

"Yes, ma'am," Becky said, feeling her cheeks burn. "You see, Woody offered to marry me to save me from spinsterhood. It made me mad, so I told him I couldn't marry him because I was already engaged."

Having worn the tag "spinster" herself up until just a few weeks before, Miss Manie humphed and settled her arms over her ample breasts. "There's nothing wrong with a woman choosing to remain single."

"I know that, but it was the way he offered the proposal that made me mad. He made it sound like he was doing me a favor or something."

Miss Manie eyed Becky suspiciously over the upper half of her bifocals. "If he'd offered a proper proposal, you'd have said yes, without batting an eye, wouldn't you?"

Becky's second "yes, ma'am" was barely audible.

Miss Manie leaned closer and placed a knuckle under Becky's chin, forcing her to meet her gaze. "No need to be embarrassed about your feelings, Rebecca Lee. You're among friends here."

Becky firmed her lips to keep the tears at bay. "Thank you, Miss Manie."

Miss Manie sat back in her chair, studying Becky. "So how did Forrest accept the news of your fiancé?"

"Well," Becky began slowly, "I don't think he be-

lieved me, because he started asking me all these questions about where I met him, what his name was. He was
shooting questions at me so fast, that I don't remember
half of what I told him.'' She sank back against her chair
in disgust. ''Then, this evening, he came over and told
me that he wanted to run a trace on my fiancé, just to
make sure the guy was on the up-and-up. And the worst
of it is,'' she added, her voice rising in frustration, ''he's
been telling it all over town that I'm engaged.'' Becky
closed her fingers around the edge of the table and pulled
herself forward. ''What am I going to do, Miss Manie?''
she cried. ''I've dug myself so deep in the lie, I can't see
the light.''

''Before I can advise you, I need to know why you told
the lie.''

''I told you, I was mad.''

''Yes, I imagine you were,'' Miss Manie agreed read-
ily, ''and justifiably so. But why did you tell Forrest that
you were engaged? Why not just refuse his proposal out-
right?''

''Because he made me sound like a charity case, and I
wanted to prove to him that I wasn't.''

Miss Manie arched a pointed brow, waiting. ''And...''

Becky ducked her head. ''Well, I suppose I might have
wanted to make him a little jealous, too.''

''Now we're getting to the crux of the matter,'' Miss
Manie said, pursing her lips in smug satisfaction. ''And
did you succeed?''

Becky slowly shook her head. ''I don't think so.''

''I do,'' Callie piped in, then quickly pressed her fingers
to her lips, blushing a pretty shade of pink as she glanced
Becky's way. ''Sorry. I didn't mean to stick my nose in
where it's not welcome.''

Becky waved away the apology. "Stick your nose in as far as you want. I need all the help I can get."

Callie leaned forward, obviously enjoying being a part of the conversation. "In that case, I think Forrest's curiosity about your fiancé was a sure sign of jealousy. Otherwise, he wouldn't care enough to ask questions. Wouldn't you agree, Aunt Manie?" she asked, looking to her aunt for approval.

"I would."

Becky tossed up her hands. "Great. So he's jealous. What do I do now? Just tell him the truth and suffer the consequences?"

"Eventually," Manie said thoughtfully while she stirred her tea. After a moment, she set aside her spoon. "But first, he needs to stew for a while. It'll do the boy good."

"I don't think I follow you," Becky said, puzzled.

"Play this fiancé of yours up for a while," Miss Manie suggested. "Let Forrest go on thinking you are already taken. See how he reacts. It might force his hand."

"Force his hand?" Becky repeated, more confused than before. "In what way?"

"If Forrest thinks he's going to lose you to another man," Miss Manie explained, "he might just decide to put up a fight for you. A fight," she added, chuckling, "that you're going to let him win."

Three

Yawning, Forrest dropped down in the leather wing chair, then swung his legs up and propped his boot heels on his oversize mahogany desk. Taking a careful sip of his coffee, he glanced toward the darkened window, a reminder that he was up before the sun again. Not that he needed the reminder. He hadn't gotten a full night's rest since he'd returned from the mission trip to Europe. This wife-picking business was beginning to wear on his nerves, he thought irritably.

Out of habit, he picked up his little black book, thumbed through a couple of pages, studying the names listed there, then tossed down the worn book with a muttered curse. There was no use in looking through the names again. He'd already ruled out every woman he'd ever had a date with.

And the one woman he *hadn't* ever dated had ruled *him* out.

He frowned, rubbing a hand at the sudden stab of pain in his chest. He wasn't suffering from a broken heart, he told himself firmly. Hell, it wasn't as if Becky had jilted him or anything. His proposal to her had been more like a business deal. Yeah, that was it, he thought, warming to the idea. He needed a wife and children, and Becky needed a husband and someone to take care of her. A fair exchange to his way of thinking.

Only the deal hadn't gelled, he reminded himself grimly.

Becky was engaged to somebody else and Forrest was right back where he started, needing a wife.

He took a careful sip of his coffee, then laid his head back with a sigh, feeling the first kick of caffeine to his system. Balancing his mug on his belt buckle, he settled his gaze on the far wall and the framed pictures hanging there—pictures of family and friends, favorite horses, a couple of prized bulls the Cunningham's had raised over the years. Though twenty or more photographs hung there, one in particular caught his eye—a portrait of the Cunningham family taken twenty years before.

As he stared at the family portrait, memories of the day he and his parents had posed for the photograph pushed aside his concerns about finding himself a wife.

He'd just turned sixteen when his mother had insisted they needed a family portrait to commemorate the event and had arranged for a photographer from Midland to drive to their ranch so the pictures could be taken in their home. She had strong-armed Forrest into getting a fresh haircut for the occasion, and had even laid out the clothes she had wanted him to wear for the sitting. He chuckled, recalling the fight that had ensued over her selection.

More comfortable in jeans and boots, he had balked at the idea of putting on the coat and tie she had chosen,

claiming that suits were reserved for marrying and burying. Since nobody had died, he'd informed her, and since
he wasn't planning on getting married anytime soon, he
didn't see any reason why he should have to wear the
dang thing. They had argued for half an hour or more
before his mother had finally stormed out of his room,
muttering that he wouldn't have to worry about wearing
a suit to get married in because no woman in her right
mind would ever have him, but that he might very well
be wearing a suit to a funeral—his own—because she was
about a hair away from strangling him.

He chuckled again as he focused in on his mother's
image. Kathleen Cunningham might look like a spa-
pampered woman, but she was a tough old bird, and could
give as good as she got. Her one disappointment in life,
by her own admission, was that she hadn't been able to
fill the house her husband had built for her with the children she'd wanted so badly. Though she loved the only
son she'd been blessed with, and never hesitated to dem-
onstrate that affection whether in public or private, she
doled out discipline in the same open manner. From the
day she'd given birth to Forrest, she'd sworn that he
wouldn't be spoiled, and she'd personally done everything
in her power to see that he wasn't. As soon as he was big
enough to prop up in a saddle, she'd insisted that her
husband take Forrest with him when he rode out over their
ranch, checking the cattle and the windmills.

Remembering those rides, Forrest shifted his gaze to
the man who stood beside his mother, one broad, tanned
hand resting on her slender shoulder. A tall man, solidly
built, Newt Cunningham had done his own part to see that
Forrest wasn't coddled. He'd demanded a full day's work
from his son, the same as he did from the wranglers on
his payroll, and would accept nothing less. In the process,

he had instilled in Forrest a strong work ethic, a love for the ranch that would be his one day, and had taught him everything he'd need to know about running it.

Though he'd never received more than a high school degree himself, Newt Cunningham had insisted that Forrest go to college. He had also been instrumental in Forrest's decision to serve a stint in the military, having taught his son from an early age that it was a man's duty to serve his country when the time came. As a result, after college, Forrest had traded his Stetson for a green beret and served his time in the armed forces gathering military intelligence in foreign countries.

The knowledge and experience he had gained both at the university and abroad came in handy eight years earlier when his parents had suddenly announced that they were retiring and were turning the management of the ranch over to him. With nothing more than a pat on the back and a wave goodbye, they'd moved to Midland and their new home there, leaving Forrest alone in the big rambling house he'd grown up in.

Alone.

Frowning at the reminder, he rubbed a thoughtful thumb along the side of his coffee mug. In the beginning, being alone had suited him just fine. Then, he'd been busy…okay, maybe a little obsessed, he amended at his conscience's nudging…in proving that his parent's trust in him was well-placed. But his hard work had paid off. He'd taken an already successful cattle ranch and parlayed it into a billion dollar corporation by investing its profits in oil and real estate, making him one of the wealthiest cattle barons in the world.

But he didn't want to be alone any longer. He wanted a wife and kids.

Feeling the blue mood edging its way back over him

and determined to fight it off, he forced his gaze to another picture, this one taken at one of the annual barbecues held on the Golden Steer. Linen-covered tables were scattered all around the flagstone patio that fanned from the ranch house at the Golden Steer's headquarters. Above them, strings of miniature lights twinkled from the patio's ivy-draped lattice roof. Smoke billowed from the oversize grill built into the patio's low rock wall, where a much younger Forrest and two wranglers tended slow-cooking briskets, prime beef raised and butchered right on the Golden Steer.

The photographer had captured the guests, smiling and talking in small groups, just as the sun was setting. Forrest recognized a United States senator among them, a *New York Times* bestselling author, a professional football player, as well as neighbors and family friends. He chuckled when he singled Becky from the crowd, dressed in her usual attire of jeans and boots, her mane of hair a flame of red against the darkening Texas sky.

He moved his gaze from one picture to another, lost in the memories each drew...and slowly became aware that one person appeared in nearly every one of the framed shots.

Becky Sullivan.

He shifted his gaze back to the family portrait. She wasn't in that picture, but he remembered her being there that day, standing off to the side, making faces at him and trying to make him laugh.

His throat tightened as he stared at the wall of pictures and the events and the memories each represented. Becky as a young girl, standing beside him in front of the Cunningham family Christmas tree, the sorrow over the loss of her mother still evident in her big, green eyes. A teenaged Becky with a ponytail and an attitude all decked out in Western finery, riding one of the Cunninghams' cutting horses in a state competition. Becky on her twenty-first birthday, grinning and holding her first legal beer high in the air.

He rubbed a hand across his chest, the ache returning with a vengeance. Becky Sullivan was as much a part of his life as his parents were.

But she wouldn't be for much longer. She was getting married. And she'd be moving away, leaving him behind, just as his parents had.

Groaning, he dropped his boots to the floor, then leaned to set his coffee mug on his desk. With his elbows braced on his knees, he buried his face in his hands. He didn't want to lose Becky. Hell, she was like a sister to him. A best friend.

You can take your friendly offer to run a trace on my fiancé, get the heck off of my land, and stay off.

Remembering her angry command, he collapsed against the chair's soft leather back, realizing that he might very well have already lost her friendship, if not her physically. Instead of offering her congratulations on her engagement and upcoming marriage, he'd all but called her a liar and belittled the man she'd chosen to marry. And what kind of person would do a thing like that to a friend?

A selfish one, he told himself in disgust.

An apology was due, but admitting a wrong had never come easy for Forrest. Firming his lips, he pushed out of the chair and to his feet. He'd apologize this time, though, he promised himself as he reached for his hat. And maybe—if he was lucky—Becky would find it in her heart to forgive him his callous behavior. And if she didn't…

He slammed the back door behind him with a little more force than was needed. Well, she *would* forgive him, because he wasn't leaving the Rusty Corral until she did.

Becky dumped feed into the mare's trough, then crossed back to the bin and filled the bucket again.

Woody fight for me?

She snorted as she tossed the scoop back into the bin, remembering Miss Manie's prediction from the night before. Miss Manie was a wise woman, and one whom Becky loved dearly, but this time she was wrong. Dead wrong. Becky couldn't imagine Woody fighting another man for her hand in marriage.

Especially an invisible man.

She grimaced at the reminder of the lie she'd told. A fiancé. Of all the reasons she could have offered to Woody for not marrying him, why did she have to fabricate a fiancé? Huffing a disgusted breath, she lifted the bucket, carried it to the last stall and dumped the feed into the trough.

With all the livestock fed and her morning chores done, she hooked the bucket's handle over a nail and headed for the house and her own breakfast, cursing her stupidity every step of the way.

"A fiancé," she muttered. "Of all the stupid, harebrained things to come up with."

On the back stoop, she faltered, one hand clasped around the door handle. The thought of entering the house and eating another solitary meal had her dropping her hand and sinking down on the top step in dejection. She was tired of eating alone. Of sleeping alone. Heck, of just *being* alone!

But, by the look of things, she was going to be alone for a long, long time.

She wrapped her arms around her legs, hugging them to her chest. With her chin propped on her knees, she watched the sky bleed with dawn's awakening colors. In the distance, she could hear the low call of cattle, the lonesomeness in the sound intensified by her own melancholy mood.

It was at times like this that she missed her mother the most, she thought sadly. The quiet times, the lonely times. The times when a hug and an encouraging word were needed most. Though her mother had died when Becky was only seven, she still remembered her. The way she smiled. Her laugh. Her scent. The hugs she passed out like cookies that were just as sweet and twice as filling.

But her mother was gone. And for all practical purposes, so was her dad. She snorted a laugh as she thought of Shorty Sullivan. A dreamer. That's what her father was. Always chasing after the horse that would put him on easy street. The one that would earn him the reputation as the best horse trainer in Texas, or the long shot that crossed the finish line first. After years of chasing, Shorty still hadn't found that horse, but he'd never quit looking, never quit dreaming.

A wet nose bumped against her arm and she glanced over to find Rowdy, Woody's cow dog, beside her.

"Hey, Rowdy," she said, reaching to scruff him between the ears. "How ya doin', buddy?"

He barked, then butted his nose against her arm. He whined low in his throat and looked at her expectantly, his tongue lolling out of the side of his mouth.

She laughed. "Wanting some breakfast, are you?"

"Don't beg, Rowdy."

Becky snapped her head around to find Woody standing at the side of the house, holding the reins of his favorite gelding loosely in his hand. She had been afraid that he wouldn't show up today—or any day in the future, for that matter—since she'd so rudely ordered him off her land the night before.

But there he was, bigger than life, and looking more

handsome that any man deserved. He was dressed in his work clothes—jeans and leather chaps, a faded chambray shirt and boots with more scuff than shine. A battered cowboy hat set low over his forehead shadowed his face. In the haze of dawn's early light, he looked like a cow-poke straight out of the Old West who'd made a wrong turn along the way and somehow wound up in the twentieth century.

Though Woody was a wealthy man and had closets full of custom-made shirts and suits, and boots of every color and description, Becky always preferred seeing him dressed this way. For some reason, it made her feel on more equal footing with him. She supposed that it was ridiculous to feel that way, since Woody's family owned the biggest ranch in West Texas and had more money than they could spend in a lifetime, while her own family lived more a hand-to-mouth existence.

While she stared at him, he cleared his throat and shifted uneasily from one foot to the other. Embarrassed, she quickly pushed to her feet and dusted off the seat of her jeans. "It's my fault Rowdy was begging. I gave him biscuits every morning while you were gone. I guess he's grown to expect them."

Without bothering to reply, Woody tied his horse to a hitching post set near the back porch, then turned, pulling off his hat. He held it between his hands as he met her gaze. The graveness in his expression and the fact that he didn't draw any closer had Becky's stomach tightening in dread.

Had he come to fire her? she wondered as a new worry jumped to life to gnaw at her. Not that she'd blame him, if he did, considering the way she'd yelled at him and ordered him off her land. She gave herself a swift mental kick. If she lost her one sure source of income, it would be her own darn fault. But, dang it! She needed the pay-check she drew from the Golden Steer each month, and wasn't sure how she'd make ends meet if she no longer had that income to rely on.

While she mentally castigated herself, he cleared his throat again as if what he was preparing to say pained him somehow.

"I don't believe I ever got around to offering you my congratulations yesterday," he said gruffly.

The relief Becky should have felt when he didn't fire her wasn't there. Guilt over the lie she'd told slipped in to replace it. Knowing full well *she* should be the one doing the apologizing, she stammered, "N-no, you didn't."

"Well, I'm sorry about that, and my rudeness."

"No apology needed."

She watched the tenseness ease out of his shoulders as he settled his hat back on his head. Warily she watched him as he walked toward her, sure that he had more to say. "Is that all?"

He stopped, his brow furrowing in puzzlement. "Well, yeah, unless there's something else I need to apologize for."

"No!" she said quickly. "No, there's nothing else."

"I'm forgiven, then?"

"Yeah," she said uneasily, that guilt eating a little deeper, "I guess so."

He grinned then, and pressed a hand against the small of her back and aimed her for the door. "Good, 'cause Rowdy and me were hoping we could talk you into fixing us some breakfast."

She frowned at him over her shoulder as she opened the back door. "Times must be hard over at the Golden Steer if both you and your dog are begging."

"Nope," he said, his grin widening. "You're just a better cook than me."

Becky bit back a smile. "A fact that you take advantage of every chance you get."

"My mama didn't raise a fool," he said with a wink.

Once inside, he took off his hat and hung it on the pegged rack by the door. "So what's for breakfast?"

"Whatever I decide to put on the table, and no complaining."

"Have I ever?"

"No, but there's always a first time." She washed her hands and dried them as she headed for the refrigerator. "You're out early this morning."

He pulled out a chair at the table and made himself at home. "Thought I'd ride along with you today while you check the windmills."

She glanced his way as she cracked eggs. "Don't trust me to do the job?"

"I didn't say I was going to double-check your work. I just said I was going to ride along. We lost a couple of steers last week."

Grease popped as she poured the egg batter into the hot skillet. "Coyotes?"

"Probably." He reared back in his chair, tipping it back on two legs, and watched her. "I thought I'd check for tracks, see how many we're dealing with."

"Are you going to organize a hunt?"

"Not if I can handle it myself."

She shrugged, knowing that was Woody's way. He seldom sought the help of outsiders when he could do the work himself. "I'll help out, if you want."

"I was counting on it."

She tossed a teasing grin over her shoulder. "It'll cost you, though."

Relieved ·that Becky seemed to harbor no ill feelings toward him, Forrest slipped easily into the game, one that they had played often over the years. They always dickered over the value of her services, with Becky suggesting items in exchange for her labor, while Forrest groaned and complained about how she was going to send him to the poor house. In the end, he usually gave her what she wanted. "How much?"

Becky turned back to her stirring. "Oh, I don't know. That new mare's foal ought to about cover my expenses."

"What!" All four legs of his chair hit the floor with a thump. "That mare's a registered quarter horse and that foal she's carrying was sired by the most high-powered stud in Colorado."

Becky just smiled as she scooped scrambled eggs onto a plate. "The mare might be registered," she conceded as she plunked a couple of cold biscuits on his plate, "and the sire might be some high-powered stud—" she crossed to him and set the plate down in front of him, then stepped back and folded her arms over her breasts "—but that foal hasn't proven itself, yet."

Forrest scowled at her as he whipped a napkin across his lap. "Proven or not, that foal is worth thousands."

Becky's smile widened, her green eyes twinkling. "And so am I."

At that point in the negotiations, in the past, Forrest would ordinarily have snorted and offered her something else, like a bag of oats or a couple of bales of alfalfa hay. Something she needed, something she could use. But as he stared into those laughing green eyes of hers, all he could think about was that she was getting married and that this might very well be the last time he ate breakfast at her house, or had the chance to barter with her for her services.

"Where are you going to live?"

Expecting his usual smart comeback to her claim of worth, Becky looked at him in confusion. "What?"

He tore his gaze from hers and picked up his fork. "Where are you and your husband going to live after y'all get married?"

Her smile slowly faded and she quickly turned away. "I don't know. We haven't discussed that, yet." She felt his gaze on her back as she scraped eggs onto her plate.

"Do you think you'll stay on here? I doubt Shorty would care."

She lifted a shoulder, but kept her back to him. "Maybe. I don't know." Mentally she gave herself another kick for allowing her pride to get her in this mess. But she couldn't see a way free of it, not without telling him the truth, something Miss Manie had advised against. She drew in a deep shuddering breath. She could play this out, she told herself. All she had to do was string Woody along for a while. Just long enough to force his hand. Just until he was willing to offer the proposal she wanted to hear.

She pasted on a smile and turned for the table. "Joe doesn't really care one way or the other, so we might stay on here."

"Joe?" he repeated, glancing up at her. "I thought you said your fiancé's name was John?"

"Oh, it is!" she said quickly and dropped onto the chair opposite him. "John. John Smythe. With a *y* instead of an *i* and with—"

"—an *e* at the end," he finished for her. "So why'd you call him Joe?"

She flapped a hand and laughed self-consciously. "It's just a little nickname I have for him."

"And what does he call you?"

"H-he—" Thankfully the phone rang at that moment, saving her from having to come up with an answer. She stretched a hand behind her to snag it from the wall unit. "Hello?"

"Good morning, Rebecca Lee."

Becky's brows shot up in surprise at the sound of Miss Manie's voice. "What are you doing calling me so early?"

"I wanted to catch you before you left for the day and see if you could arrange to be home around one."

Becky glanced across the table at Woody who had stopped eating and was watching her curiously. "Well, I don't know. Woody's here right now and as soon as we finish breakfast, we're heading out to check the windmills."

"He's there by the phone?"

"Yeah," Becky replied slowly. "Why?"

"Does he know it's me on the line?"

Becky studied Woody's expression. "I don't think so."

"Good. Pretend that I'm your fiancé."

Becky suppressed a groan and pressed a hand to her forehead, feeling a headache coming on. "Oh, I don't know if I can do that," she said weakly.

"Sure you can," Miss Manie assured her. "Just say whatever comes to mind and throw in a honey or a darling now and then."

"But—"

"No 'buts,' Rebecca Lee. You want to make him jealous, don't you?"

"Yeah. I guess so."

"Then say it."

Becky pressed the phone closer to her cheek and stole a quick glance at Woody. "Okay," she said into the receiver, then added, "If you say so…honey."

"Excellent! Is he listening?"

Becky stole another look at Woody. "Yeah."

"Does he look happy or mad?"

"I'd say the latter," she replied uneasily, and quickly looked away from his thunderous expression.

"Say something really suggestive."

"Like what?"

"Heavens, Rebecca Lee! Don't you ever watch television or read any books?"

"No...uh, darling, I don't."

"For pity's sake!" Miss Manie grumped. "What do you do at night? Oh, never mind," she said before Becky could answer. "Just ask me what I'm doing."

"What are you doing?"

"Try to make your voice softer. More playful. And tell me how you wish you were with me right now."

Becky felt her cheeks burn, but couldn't seem to push a word past the lump in her throat.

"Rebecca! Say it!"

Becky put a hand above her brow, shading her eyes from Woody, then cleared her throat. "I wish I were with you right now."

"Oh, excellent! Excellent! Is he still listening?"

Becky peeked through a slit in her fingers and swallowed hard at the murderous look in Woody's eyes. "Yeah."

"Well, let's not press our luck. Say you love me and then we'll hang up."

Becky turned her back to Woody, closed her eyes and took a deep breath. "I love you."

She heard a chair scrape against the floor behind her, and glanced around in time to see Woody slap a palm against the screen door. His growl of, "I'll be outside" was followed by the slamming of the door.

"What was that noise?" Miss Manie demanded to know.

"It was Woody leaving. Oh, Miss Manie," Becky whispered anxiously, craning her neck to see what he was doing. "I don't think I can go through with this."

"Sure you can. Now be home by one. I'm having something delivered to your house. Bye, dear."

"Miss Manie, wait!" Becky cried. But there was no reply. Just a click in her ear then a dial tone.

She slowly stood and replaced the receiver, then combed both hands through her hair, holding it back from her face. "Oh, Lord," she murmured shakily. "I'm not sure I'm cut out for this romantic playacting stuff."

"How many?" Becky asked.

Hunkered down on the ground, Woody examined the tracks. "Four or five," he replied tersely, then rose and swung up into his saddle. Without so much as a glance in Becky's direction, he spurred his horse on.

He'd been acting that way all morning, speaking only when spoken to, his answers brief to the point of rudeness.

Becky watched him ride away from her, her heart sinking. Miss Manie's wrong on this one, she told herself. He's not jealous, he's mad. Damn mad.

But why? she cried silently. She hadn't done anything to him…other than lie, of course, but he didn't know that. The fact that he was being so rude nudged her own temper up a notch and made her determined to follow Miss Manie's suggestion, if for no other reason than to spite him.

She turned her horse to follow him. "Woody?"

"What?"

"What time is it?"

He huffed a breath, but lifted his wrist. "Twelve-thirty. You taking medicine or something?" .

She kicked her horse into a trot to catch up with him. "No. But I've got to be home by one."

He twisted his head around to scowl at her. "Why? Is your *fiancé* coming over?"

The inflection he put on "fiancé" irritated Becky. She was getting a little tired of his sour attitude. Especially considering how this whole mess was his fault, not hers. If he'd asked her to marry him properly, instead of making the proposal sound like he was doing her a favor, she'd never have had to make up the fiancé in the first place. "No," she replied, with a haughty lift of her chin. "I'm expecting a delivery."

"Fine," he grated out. "We'll check forty-six and head home."

"I don't need your help," she snapped in return. "I can check the pump myself." She kicked her horse into a lope and raced across the pasture, ducking her head against the wind to avoid the stinging granules of sand it carried. She dodged the occasional mesquite, scared a jackrabbit from a clump of grease wood, and by the time she reached forty-six, the wind had cooled her temper somewhat. She swung down from her saddle and looped her reins around the leg of the windmill's tower. She checked to see that the pump was working, then moved on to check the water level in the reservoir.

At the sound of hoof beats, she glanced up to see that Woody had followed her. Frowning, she turned her back on him and dipped her hands in the pool. She splashed water over her face, washing away the grit the wind had left there, then untied the bandanna from around her throat and blotted the moisture from her face.

"Everything okay?" he asked as he swung down from his saddle.

"Fine," she replied, without looking at him.

She heard the scrape of his boots on the loose rock, then he was standing beside her. "Sorry if I was short with you," he muttered as he leaned to brace his hands on the edge of the reservoir.

Two apologies in one day? Shocked, Becky stared at his back as he ducked his head beneath the water. He came up growling and shaking water from his hair like a dog.

Without thinking, she passed him her bandanna.

"Thanks," he mumbled and scrubbed the bandanna over his face, wiping off the water and, along with it, an accumulation of sweat and sand. When he was done, he cocked his head to look at her, one eye narrowed. "You gonna feed me lunch?"

She pursed her lips and glared right back at him. "I suppose," she said grudgingly.

He passed her back the bandanna. "Good. I'm starving." Then, to her surprise, he hooked an arm around her neck, and turned her around, guiding her back to their horses.

As quick as that, she thought in frustration. He's mad, then he's glad. She was having a hard time keeping up with his violent mood swings.

"I figure we'll start tracking the coyotes tomorrow. It'll probably take us a couple of days to cover the area, so we'll need to camp out." He dropped his arm from around her and untied her reins. "Will you have a problem with that?" he asked, passing them to her.

"No."

In the process of untying his own horse, he angled his head to look over at her. "No date?"

Becky felt the anger rise and fought to tamp it down. "No."

He nodded, seemingly satisfied with her answer, then swung up in the saddle. "Race you," he challenged and dug his spurs into his horse's sides.

Still on the ground, Becky yelled after him. "Dang you, Woody! That's not fair. You got a head start." Cursing him under her breath, she grabbed for her horn, swung up into the saddle and took out after him.

Woody's horse was bred for speed and endurance, but Becky's was just as quick and loved nothing better than to run. Within seconds she'd narrowed the distance between them. Another few seconds and she was confident she was within range. Slipping her lariat from around her saddle horn, she shook out a loop. She circled it twice over her head, eyeing her target, then let it fly. The hand-smoothed hemp whooshed through the air, then settled cleanly over Woody's head, dropping around his arms. Startled, he jerked back on his reins and his horse sat back on his haunches, churning dust. Becky sailed past them. "Cheater," she accused, then grinned and tossed him the end of the rope.

"Gawldang you, Becky Lee," he yelled after her.

She just tossed back her head and laughed and raced on.

Fighting and cussing as he fought free of the rope, he spurred his horse again. "You're gonna regret that," he warned.

"You gotta catch me first," she called over her shoulder, still laughing.

And the race was on.

By the time they reached the Rusty Corral, their horses were nose-to-nose...but Becky was the first to hit the ground. She ran to the house, slapping a hand against the weathered wood, the signal for a win they'd developed years ago. Her face flushed with victory, she turned to grin up at him. "Beatcha."

"Did not," he argued and swung down from his saddle. "You cheated."

"You cheated first!" she cried indignantly. "You got a head start, so that makes us even." She folded her arms stubbornly over her breasts. "Admit it, Woody, I won fair and square."

Growling low in his throat, he dropped his reins and started toward her, his eyes narrowed, his hands poised at his sides like a gunslinger.

Becky started backing up. "Now, Woody…" she began.

He ignored her plea, and kept coming.

She giggled, stumbled, then quickly regained her balance, holding out a hand to ward him off. "Come on, Woody. You know I won. Admit it."

She yelped when he made a lunge for her, and turned to run…but she was too late. His arms caught her around the thighs, and then she was falling. She hit the ground face first, eating dirt, but before she could draw the first breath, he'd flipped her over and she was looking up at the sky. She had time to gulp in one breath, then he was straddling her and had her arms pinned above her head.

He was breathing hard, his chest pumping against hers as rhythmically as the oil derricks that dotted the Golden Steer. His face was so close she could feel the warm moistness of his breath on her cheek, count the squint lines that fanned from the corners of his eyes.

"Who did you say won?" he challenged.

She thrashed beneath him, trying to break his hold, but he simply tightened his fingers around her wrists.

Seemingly satisfied with his dominant position, he

smiled smugly and shifted his weight. At the movement, his chest chafed across her breasts. He froze at the unexpected contact. Becky watched his eyes sharpen with awareness, then slowly darken. He shifted again, purposefully this time, his chest rubbing across her breasts. Once. Twice. Three times. His eyes drilling a hole all the way to her soul. What she saw in the brown depths stole what was left of her breath. Heat. A burning heat so intense she felt as if she'd been branded by it. She couldn't have moved if her life had depended on it.

And Forrest couldn't stop moving. With each slow rock of his body over hers, he became aware of another part of her femininity. The swells of her breasts, the tightly budded nipples, the twin hills of pelvic bone that poked at his groin.

"Becky," he began, his voice sounding desperate and needy even to his own ears. "I—"

Beep! Beep!

He twisted his head around at the unexpected sound and watched as a white van pulled to a stop in front of the house. Painted a garish yellow, a stripe on the truck's side panel read, Dee Dee's Bouquets.

He dropped his chin to his chest and swore.

A door slammed and a voice called out, "Yahoo! Becky? Is that you underneath Forrest?"

Forrest lifted his head to meet Becky's gaze. She stared back at him, wide-eyed, her lips trembling.

"Y-yeah," she stammered, then more loudly, "Yeah, Dee Dee, it's me."

A pair of three-inch heels and a stretch of bare leg appeared in Forrest's peripheral vision, then Dee Dee was squatting down on the ground beside them, balancing a huge vase of roses on her knees. She stuck her face in the space between theirs, looking at first one then the other.

She beamed a smile bright enough to snag a job for a toothpaste commercial. "Aren't you two a little old to be wrestling around on the ground?" she chided teasingly.

Slowly Forrest released his hold on Becky's wrists and levered himself to his feet. His gaze on Becky's, he reached down and offered her his hand. "I was just teaching Becky a new self-defense technique." He kept his gaze on hers, daring her to disagree with him.

"Y-yeah," she stammered, accepting the hand up. She made a show of dusting off her jeans and shirt. "That was a good one, Woody," she improvised. "Caught me totally off guard."

Dee Dee giggled and stood, too, easing up beside Forrest. "You'll have to teach me that move, Forrest." She shifted the vase to her hip and balanced it there, so she could free a hand to loop through his arm. She snuggled close, pressing one of her 36DD's against his arm as she looked up and batted her false eyelashes at him. "A girl never knows when she might have to defend herself against an aggressive male."

Becky huffed a disbelieving breath. "As if you'd put up a fight," she muttered under her breath as she stooped to scrape her hat from the ground.

Forrest carefully peeled the woman's fingers from around his arm and stepped away, separating himself from her. "Sure, Dee Dee. Anytime." He nodded toward the vase of roses. "What have you got there?"

Dee Dee smiled up at him. "Roses. For Becky," she added with a can-you-believe-it arch of one brow, then turned to offer them to her.

Becky accepted them with a mumbled thanks, her cheeks burning with embarrassment. *I'm gonna kill you, Miss Manie,* she threatened silently.

Dee Dee edged closer, her gaze straying to the card

buried among the roses. "Everybody at the shop is just dying to know who sent them."

Sure that Dee Dee had known all along that Miss Manie was the one who had ordered the flowers, Becky looked up at her in surprise. "You don't know?"

"Uh-uh. The order arrived by special courier earlier this morning. There was an envelope with instructions and cash inside, but there was no name anywhere and the enclosure card was sealed. Not that we would have looked," she added quickly, glancing up at Becky, all innocence. Then she turned her gaze on the card again, eyeing it like a druggy would his next fix. "Aren't you going to open it?" she asked hopefully, then flapped her hand, and laughed. "Well, of course you're not! Your hands are full."

Before Becky could stop her, Dee Dee had plucked the small envelope from among the roses, slipped a nail beneath the flap and was pulling out the enclosed card. She quickly scanned it, her eyes widening. She lifted her head to stare at Becky in surprise. "Oh-h-h, my!"

Forrest moved closer, his curiosity overruling good sense. "Who sent them?"

Dee Dee fanned her face with the card. "I don't know, but I sure would like to meet him." She lifted a questioning brow at Becky. "Is he as good in bed as he is with words?"

Becky snatched the card from Dee Dee's hand, then gave the woman a nudge with her elbow. "I don't want to keep you, Dee Dee. I'm sure you've got other deliveries to make. Thanks for bringing the flowers out."

"Yeah," Dee Dee said, casting a regretful look Forrest's way, "I do have a few other stops to make." With a sigh, she turned for her van, churning her hips from side to side—for Woody's benefit, Becky was sure. When she reached the van, she turned and waved at him. "Now don't you forget that you promised to teach me that self-defense move," she called.

"I won't, Dee Dee."

"Tramp," Becky muttered under her breath.

He turned to look at her. "What?"

She shifted the vase in her arms. "I said, cramp. Holding these roses is making my arm cramp."

Reminded of the flowers, Forrest shifted his gaze to them. He wanted to ask who they were from, what the card said. But he knew who'd sent them. Becky's fiancé. And he didn't think he wanted to know what the card said. Not after witnessing Dee Dee's reaction to it.

And after feeling Becky lying beneath him, her breasts pressed against his chest, the thought of her in bed with another man...well, it just plain made him sick.

He nodded toward the flowers. "Better get 'em in the house before the wind beats all the petals off," he said gruffly. He stooped and scraped his hat from the ground where it had fallen and settled it back over his head, then headed for his horse. "See you later," he mumbled miserably.

"Hey! What about lunch?" Becky called after him. "I thought you were starving?"

He stopped beside his horse and gathered up the reins. Swinging up into the saddle, he muttered, "Not anymore," and turned the gelding for home.

Four

"**W**as he there when the roses were delivered?"

Becky stuffed an armload of quilts into a box and pressed them down with a little more force than necessary. "Oh, he was there, all right," she replied dryly as she stretched to grab a roll of packing tape from the floor.

Miss Manie closed the top of the now empty cedar chest and dusted off her hands. "What was his reaction?"

Scowling, Becky fought with the strip of tape she'd dispensed. "He climbed on his horse and left."

"Perfect."

"Perfect?" Becky echoed, frowning as she slung her hand, trying to shake loose from the sticky tape.

Chuckling, Miss Manie snipped the strip free from the roll, then unwound the mangled tape from Becky's fingers. "Yes, perfect," she repeated. She gestured toward the box. "Hold the lid down," she instructed, "and I'll tape it shut."

Becky pressed her hands against the lid. "What's so good about him leaving? I thought the idea was to keep him around so that I could make him jealous?"

With a soft creak of her knees, Miss Manie straightened and brushed the back of her wrist across her forehead, pushing back her gray hair. "That was just the first stage of our plan. Now it's time for stage two." She waved her hand at the box they'd sealed. "Just set it there by the door with the others."

Struggling to lift the cumbersome box, Becky eyed Miss Manie warily. "I don't think I want to know what stage two is."

"You want Forrest to fight for you, don't you?"

Becky shoved the box on top of the growing pile by the door. "Fight who? A shadow?"

"Never you mind," Miss Manie said, wagging a stern finger at Becky. "It's the intent we're after, not the act."

Weary of talking about the mess she'd gotten herself in, Becky glanced around the nearly empty room. "What's next?"

Miss Manie looked around, too, and bit down on her lip to stop its quivering.

"*Aww,* now, Miss Manie," Becky soothed, moving to wrap an arm around the older woman's shoulder. "You're not going to cry, are you?"

Miss Manie gave a quick sniff. "Piddle. Why would I cry? It's just an old house."

Becky chuckled and gave her a squeeze. "A house that you've lived in—for what?" she asked, peering curiously at the woman. "Forty years?"

"Forty-nine, but who's counting?" Miss Manie waved away Becky's offer of sympathy. "We've done enough packing for one day. Any more, and there won't be a thing left for that new husband of mine to do when he arrives."

She headed for the doorway. "Come on out to the kitchen and we'll have us a cup of herbal tea while I go over the steps for stage two."

Becky followed, her steps heavy with dread. "This isn't going to be like step one, is it? Where you send me flowers and I have to say mushy stuff to you on the phone?"

Miss Manie turned, frowning her disapproval over the top of her bifocals. "No. In this step, you take a much more aggressive role." Pushing her glasses up higher on her nose, she turned back to the kitchen. "It's time you started teasing him a little."

Becky stumbled to a stop, her stomach doing a slow flip. Tease him a little? Her? She hurried to catch up.

"Miss Manie, you wouldn't have a beer stashed somewhere in the house, would you?" she asked hopefully. "I think I'm going to need something a little stronger than tea before I can listen to your plans for stage two."

Forrest stood in his office, his hands braced low on his hips, staring angrily at the same wall of pictures he'd been staring at earlier that morning. Dammit! It just wasn't fair. All these years he'd spent living right next door to Becky, and he'd never once looked at her as anyone but a kid sister.

No, he corrected, pursing his lips. Not a kid sister. And that was the problem. He'd never thought of Becky in the female context, at all. He'd always looked at her more like a kid brother.

He'd wrestled with her, camped out with her, given her her first taste of beer, things he would've done with a kid brother, if he'd ever had one. Never once in all those years had he ever really thought of her as a female.

But now he did.

His cheeks puffed as he blew out a long, shaky breath.

And what a female. He'd never suspected that underneath that tough exterior Becky might be soft and curvy. But she was. And in all the right places, too. He let his head fall back with a groan, recalling the feel of her beneath him. The swell of breasts. The twin knots of aroused nipples. The flat plane of her abdomen. The hard rise of her feminine mound.

He groaned again, digging his fingers through his hair. He had no right to think of Becky in that way.

She belonged to another man.

And Forrest Cunningham never trespassed on another man's territory.

"We'll make camp here."

Becky pulled her horse to a stop beside Woody's and looked around. Moonlight spilled over the landscape, revealing a clump of squatty mesquite trees growing near a buffalo wallow. "Looks good to me." She slipped down from her horse and reached up to untie her saddlebags.

After hobbling her horse, she stripped off her gear and crossed to where Woody had already dumped his. "You want to gather the makings for a fire, or start the coffee?" she asked, dropping her saddle next to his.

Without looking at her, he mumbled, "I'll take care of the fire," then stalked off.

Becky watched him disappear into the darkness, disheartened by his foul mood. How in the world was she supposed to tease him, if he wouldn't even look at her or talk to her? She'd thought this coyote hunt would be the perfect time to implement Miss Manie's stage two, but there was only so much a woman with her lack of experience could do without a little encouragement!

With a sigh, she dug around in her saddlebags in search of the coffeepot. Using her boot as a rake, she cleared a small area for the fire, then measured grounds into the old blue enamel pot.

When Woody still hadn't returned by the time she had the coffee ready to boil, she situated their saddles near the area she'd cleared and rolled out their bedrolls. She was smoothing lumps from Woody's blanket when she heard his approaching footsteps.

She glanced up just as he squatted down to dump an armload of dead wood onto the circle of ground she'd cleared. Without a word to her, he slipped a burlap sack off his shoulder then turned the sack upside down, shaking dried cow chips over the wood. Rocking down to plant one knee on the ground, he leaned back, dug a hand into his jean pocket and fished out a butane lighter. She watched his thumb rake along the wheel and a flame jumped to life, illuminating his face.

His jaw was set hard enough to chip a tooth, she thought in frustration. But, Lordy, was he handsome. She watched as he leaned to touch the flame to the dry tender and chips, admiring the play of muscle across his back and along the length of his arm. The wood smoked for a moment, then caught. Within minutes, a fire crackled, turning his skin a burnished gold and putting a flush of red on the slash of his high cheekbones. Rugged, she decided and bit back a lustful sigh.

When the fire had burned down low enough, she set the coffeepot over it, then laid back on her bedroll, propping her spine in the curve of her saddle. Determined to put Miss Manie's plan into action, she patted the bedroll beside her. "Pull up a chair and sit awhile."

He glanced at her over his shoulder, then, with what looked like reluctance, moved to drop down beside her. He sat with his arms wrapped around his knees and stared into the fire, keeping as much distance as possible between them.

Becky frowned at his tense back. "Are you mad at me, or something?"

"No."

"Then why are you being so quiet?"

He lifted a shoulder. "Don't have anything to say, I guess."

Determined to get things underway, Becky scooted closer to the fire, until her hips were in line with his. She picked up a rock and, thoughtful, drew circles in the dirt between them. "Woody," she said after a moment, "I sort of have a problem."

He twisted his head around to look at her, his forehead furrowed in concern. "Has Shorty drained your bank account again? No need to worry, if he has. I can float you a loan till payday."

Becky shook her head, chuckling. "No. It's nothing like that." With a sigh, she tossed down the rock, and drew her legs up, hugging them to her chest as she turned her face to the fire. "It's—well—it's just..."

"Just, what?" he asked in frustration.

She turned to look at him and was struck again by his handsomeness. She'd secretly loved him for seventeen years, both as a man and as a boy, but her feelings at the moment had nothing to do with a young girl's crush, or something as hard to define as love. They were pure lust.

She had to swallow hard before she could force out the words she'd planned to say. "I'm a virgin."

She watched every muscle in his face go slack, then he whipped his head around to face the fire again, his cheeks a flaming red. "A virgin," he repeated slowly, staring at the fire.

"Yeah, a virgin."

"When did being a vir—" His voice cracked on the word and he cleared his throat, tried again. "When did, uh, being a virgin become a problem?"

"Well, it never was before, but now that I have a fiancé, it is."

"You mean," he said slowly, turning to look at her, "that you and your fiancé have never—"

"No," Becky interjected before he could say the words out loud. "We haven't."

"Does he know?"

"That I'm a virgin?" At his nod, she shook her head. "No."

He inhaled deeply then exhaled a long, shaky breath. "Is that the problem? That he doesn't know?"

"Well, sorta. See, he's coming to visit soon, and I know that we'll—well, that we'll probably do the big one," she said, unable to bring herself to say aloud the words Miss Manie had instructed her to use, "and I was wondering if you could give me some pointers."

Before she'd even completed the request, Woody was pushing out his hands and edging away from her. "No way. You're asking the wrong person. You need to talk to some woman."

"Who?" she cried in frustration. "My mother's dead and there's no one else for me to talk to. Besides," she added, "I know all about the birds and the bees. What I need are some tips on how to please a man."

"And you want *me* to give you those tips?"

"Why not? Heaven knows you've had enough experience."

Another time Forrest might have felt a swell of manly pride at the comment, but at the moment all he could think about was the irony in Becky wanting him to teach her how to please her fiancé when all evening he'd been plotting the man's death. "I don't think so, Becky."

"Why not? All you have to do is answer a few questions. What could be so hard about that?"

"What kind of questions?" he asked uneasily.

"Like, what turns a man on."

Groaning, he dropped his forehead against his knees.

Becky scooted closer, giving his shoulder a nudge with her own. "Come on, Woody. Just think for a minute. What things have women done to you that really turned you on?"

"Becky," he complained, lifting his head to look at her. "I really don't want to talk about this."

"Please, Woody?" she wheedled. "You're the only person I can ask."

"What about Sterling? Why not ask him?"

Becky propped her chin on her knees and picked up the rock again. "I never see Sterling anymore," she said miserably. "Not since he got married." It was a lie, of course, but Becky figured another little lie couldn't hurt her. Not when she was already doomed to hell for all the others she'd told Woody about this fiancé of hers.

Forrest stared at her bent head, knowing he was already lost. He never had been able to refuse Becky anything, especially when she looked as pitiful as she did now. "Oh, all right," he snapped. "Ask me your damn questions."

Becky dropped the rock and quickly scooted around until she was facing him, sitting cross-legged with her palms braced on her knees. "Okay. First question. What is the first thing that you notice about a woman?"

He took off his hat, and scratched his head, unable to look at her. "Her butt," he mumbled self-consciously. "I like a woman with a tight butt."

"Really?" she said in surprise. "Do I have a tight butt?"

He turned his face away, staring off into the darkness. "I don't know," he mumbled. "I don't ever look at your butt. At least not like *that*."

Becky choked on another laugh, then popped to her feet. She'd never seen Woody embarrassed before, and seeing him so now gave her courage she hadn't known she'd possessed. She planted her hands on her hips and turned her back to him. "So look now." She glanced over her shoulder. "Is it tight?" When he refused to look, she ordered sternly, "Woody!"

He swung his head around, took a quick glance at her rear end, then looked away again. "Yeah. It's tight."

Pleased, she dropped down beside him again. "Okay. Now, second question. Does it turn you on when a woman touches you?"

"Depends on where she touches."

"How about on your arm?"

He dropped an elbow over his knee, and turned his hat between his hands, watching its slow movement. "Depends."

"On what?"

He turned to scowl at her. "On what she's wearing when she's doing the touching." He rammed his hat back on his head. "This is ridiculous," he muttered. "I'm going to sleep." He flopped down on his back, pulling the brim of his hat over his face.

"Oh, come on, Woody," Becky begged, scooting over next to him. "Just a few more questions.

"No."

"Why?"

"Because every question you ask, I could answer with 'depends.'"

"Depends, on what?"

"On a lot of things."

"Like, what?"

He whipped off his hat to glare at her. "Like everything! The time of day. The weather. My mood. Hell, a woman could walk through my office buck naked, and if I was busy or had my mind on something else, I wouldn't even notice." He slapped the hat back over his face.

Becky's mouth fell open. "You're kidding me."

"Serious as a heart attack."

"But I thought men were on point all the time? You know, kind of like a hunting dog, sniffing out a trail."

He lifted his hat again, just high enough to see her face. "Where'd you get a crazy idea like that?"

"From you."

"Me!" he echoed, pushing himself up to one elbow. "I've never said anything like that to you in my life."

"No, but I've watched you and the other guys at the barbecues you have over at the Golden Steer. Y'all always line up by the beer keg and eyeball the women as they pass by. There's always a lot of elbowing and raised eyebrows when a woman with a good figure passes by."

He fell back against his saddle, slamming his hat over his face again. "You're nuts."

"I'm not, either!" she cried. "And if you think I believe that a woman could walk naked through your office and you not notice, then *you're* the one who's nuts, 'cause I don't believe it for one minute." She flopped to her back beside him and folded her arms stubbornly across her chest.

Slowly he pulled his hat from his face and rolled to his side to glare at her. "Whether you choose to believe it or not, it's the God's truth."

"Oh, really?" she replied, returning his glare. She

lifted a hand to the top button of her shirt and toyed with it. "So, if I were to take off my shirt right now, it wouldn't have any effect on you?"

"Nope."

"Wanna bet?"

"How much?"

"Five bucks."

Forrest snorted and waved away the offer. "Don't waste my time."

"Okay, then, Mr. Deep Pockets. You name the price."

He pursed his lips thoughtfully as he studied her. "A thousand dollars."

Becky's eyes widened in shock. "A thousand dollars! I don't have a thousand dollars to gamble."

He chuckled and rolled over onto his back. "Not too sure of your feminine charms, are you, if you're already worried about losing?"

Furious, Becky sat up. "Okay, a thousand dollars, it is—*if* you win. But if *I* win, then you have to promise to teach me everything you know about sex."

Forrest tried not to look smug. The odds were definitely in his favor. There was no way in hell that Becky was going to bare her chest to him. She was way too modest. "Okay, you got yourself a deal."

She immediately dipped her chin, and went to work. "Be prepared to lose," she muttered, tugging frantically at her shirt's top button.

Forrest watched her struggle with the button in growing horror, realizing too late his mistake. He'd forgotten the lengths that Becky would go to meet a dare. What in the hell had he been thinking when he had issued a challenge like that?

But a second mistake quickly followed the first—and this one was even more foolish.

He let his gaze slip to her hands.

She'd managed to open one button and was close to freeing a second, but so far she'd only exposed a little more of her throat and the shadowed hollow at its base. As he watched, firelight danced over the bared skin, turning it to a warm gold. The second button slipped free, revealing a strip of white cotton and a swell of breasts that rose and fell with each furious breath she took. His gaze settled on the shadowed channel that lay between. He swallowed hard at the enticing sight and tried to turn away...but discovered that he couldn't. What he wanted to do was place his lips there. Taste her. See if she tasted as sweet as she looked.

Another button slipped free.

"Becky?"

"What?" she snapped impatiently, her fingers fumbling clumsily at the next button.

"Stop."

"Oh, no," she cried furiously. "I'm not going to lose this dang bet. I'm going to prove you wrong."

Knowing that if he didn't do something, and fast, she was going to lose something more precious than a bet. Something more like her virginity. He clamped a hand over hers.

She snapped her gaze to his. "What?" she snapped angrily.

"Don't."

She jerked, trying to break free, then froze, slowly becoming aware of the desperation in the fingers that vised hers. Slower still she noticed the heat in his eyes, the intensity with which he was looking at her.

Her eyes widened in surprise. "I turned you on," she whispered in disbelief.

He jerked his hand from hers and rolled to his side, turning his back to her. "Don't be ridiculous."

She dropped to her hands and knees and crawled to peer over his shoulder. "Then why'd you make me stop?"

"Because."

"Because, why?"

"Because I don't want to look at you without your clothes on."

Feeling the sting of rejection, Becky rocked back on her heels, pulling the plackets of her shirt together in a fist.

"I won," she murmured, though she didn't feel much like a winner.

"So what?" he growled.

"So you have to make good on your end of the deal. You have to teach me everything you know about sex."

Five

Bleary-eyed from lack of sleep, Forrest pushed his way wearily through the back door of his house.

"Wipe your feet before you come inside."

He stopped cold at the sound of his mother's voice, one dusty boot on the tiled kitchen floor, the other still outside the door. "What are you doing here?"

Turning from the stove where she was frying bacon, Kathleen Cunningham planted a fist on her hip. "Well, good morning to you, too."

Knowing from his mother's tone that he'd offended her, Forrest closed the door behind him and frowned. "I didn't mean that the way it sounded. I just thought you and dad were still in London."

"We would be, but your father decided to come home early." She laughed as she rose to her toes to place a kiss on his cheek. "Said he couldn't stand being around people who couldn't speak proper English." She thumbed away the streak of lipstick she'd left on his face, and pursed her lips in displeasure when he ducked away from her hand. "And what are you so grumpy about this morning?"

He headed for the refrigerator. "I'm not grumpy."

She arched a brow. "Oh, really? Could have fooled me."

He yanked out a gallon of milk, then butted the door closed with his hip. "I'm not grumpy," he repeated defensively. "I'm tired. I've been up all night." He lifted the jug to his lips.

"Forrest..." she said, the word heavy with warning.

Milk sloshed, spilling down the front of his shirt. "Dammit, Mom!" he complained. "There's nobody here, but me. I ought to be able to drink straight out of the milk jug, if I want."

"I'm here," she reminded him and handed him a glass. "And watch your mouth. You know very well that I don't allow cursing in my presence."

He heaved a breath. Thirty-five years old and his mother still treated him like a little boy. The hell of it was, he felt like one when in her presence. "Sorry," he muttered.

She gave his cheek an affectionate pat. "You're forgiven. Just make sure it doesn't happen again, though," she warned as she turned back to her cooking, "or I'll have to wash out your mouth with soap."

Tired as he was, Forrest found the energy to chuckle.

"Where've you been all night?" she asked, then quickly amended the question. "Or do I want to know?"

"Nowhere that would shock your tender sensibilities. Just out hunting coyotes."

"Are they giving you trouble?"

He set the jug and glass on the table, then dropped wearily into a chair, rocking it back on two legs. One look from his mother, and he lowered it back to the floor. "Some. Nothing I can't handle."

"Did Becky go with you?"

He scowled as he filled the glass with milk. "Yeah."

"How's she doing?"

"Fine, I guess."

"Such a sweet girl," she remarked, smiling fondly as she transferred the bacon to a plate.

"Sweet?" Forrest snorted his disagreement.

"Yes, she's sweet," his mother insisted, then held up an egg. "Boiled or poached?"

"Fried."

"Bad for your cholesterol."

"I don't have a problem with my cholesterol."

"You will, if you don't start eating properly."

"There's nothing wrong with the way I eat."

"Heavens!" she exclaimed in consternation. "You're certainly in a foul mood this morning."

"There's nothing wrong with my mood."

"You've done nothing but grumble and grump since you walked in the back door."

"I told you, I'm tired."

"So go to bed."

"I intend to, as soon as I eat some breakfast."

With a sniff of annoyance, she spooned grease over his eggs, preparing them just the way he liked them. "You'll have to sleep in one of the guest rooms. I changed the linens on your bed and they're still in the dryer."

"You didn't need to do that. Marie takes care of the housework."

"A house needs more than a good going over once a week."

"I'm hardly ever here to make a mess. Once a week is plenty."

"You work too hard. You ought to be at home more."

He choked on a laugh. "And you think *I've* done nothing but grumble and grump?"

Lifting her chin, she scooped the eggs from the skillet and onto a plate. "I'm not grumpy. I'm a mother."

Chuckling, Forrest rose and crossed to her. He slung an arm around her shoulders and stooped to peck a kiss on her cheek. "And a good one, at that."

Her expression softened and she smiled wistfully, wrapping an arm around his waist and hugging him to her side. "I miss having you to take care of."

"Isn't taking care of dad enough to keep you busy?"

"No. I need children. Grandchildren," she corrected, and looked up at him pointedly. "When are you going to get around to giving me some?"

He heaved a sigh. "Hel-heck," he quickly amended, remembering her threat about the soap and not at all sure she wouldn't carry it out. "I don't know. Someday, I guess." He headed for the table, hoping to escape the interrogation he was sure was coming.

She followed right behind him with his plate. "Are you seeing any one special?"

He dropped down onto a chair. "No one in particular."

She set the plate in front of him. "Which is exactly your problem," she lectured as she pulled out the chair opposite him and sat down. "You need to settle down and focus on one woman."

"What woman?" he said in disgust. "There's not a woman in the entire county that I'd want to settle down with."

She plucked a linen napkin from the basket on the table and pushed it into his hand. "Surely there's someone."

"There's not. Believe me, I know."

"What about Becky?"

Forrest jerked his head up. "Becky Sullivan?"

She waved a hand at his shocked look. "Oh, I know that you're a good deal older than her, but once a person reaches adulthood, a difference in age is no longer a factor." She leaned forward and added pointedly, "And you certainly can't find fault with her, since you had a hand in raising her yourself."

Forrest dropped his gaze to his plate and scraped another helping of eggs onto his fork. "Becky's engaged," he mumbled.

Kathleen fell back against her chair, her eyes widening in surprise. "Becky's engaged? To who?"

"Some guy from Wichita."

"Well, I'll swan," she murmured. A slow smile began to curve at her lips. "Imagine that," she said dreamily. "Our little Becky getting married."

Forrest looked from his mother's smiling face to the sunny-side-up-eggs he'd just scooped, then dropped his fork to his plate in disgust. Why did everybody but him seem to be happy about Becky's upcoming marriage? He pushed back his chair and tossed his napkin to the table. "Thanks for breakfast, Mom."

"But you didn't finish eating," she cried, glancing at his plate, then back up at him. "Are you sick?"

"No. Just tired. I'm going to bed."

"Oh, all right then," she said, waving him away with her hand. "But don't sleep too long, or you won't be worth killing tonight at Sterling's party. Oh, and Forrest!" she called after him. "I steamed your tux for you. And wear the silk paisley cummerbund that I brought you back from our trip to Italy last spring. It's in your closet on the—"

Forrest closed the door of the guest room, cutting off the sound of his mother's voice.

Somehow he was going to have to produce these grand-children she wanted so badly, if for no other reason than to take the pressure off of him.

He stripped quickly and crawled between the covers, sighing his pleasure as he stretched out over the cool satin sheets.

But the second he closed his eyes, the image of Becky kneeling on her bedroll beside the campfire popped onto that theater screen behind his eyelids. Her face flushed with fury, her fingers tugging frantically at her shirt's buttons. The enticing swell of firm breasts she exposed. The shadowed valley between.

Groaning, he rolled to his stomach and buried his head under his pillow. He squeezed his eyes shut, determined to keep the image at bay.

But the image returned. That mane of red hair curtaining her flushed face as she struggled with the stubborn buttons. That first glimpse of fire-kissed flesh.

And this time Forrest was too exhausted to fight back the image.

It grew and lengthened, his imagination spinning out a different ending. Instead of closing his hand over hers and stopping her, he...

...moved to kneel in front of her. "Here. Let me," he whispered. Gently he brushed aside her hands and replaced them with his own. His gaze on hers, he unfastened each button, watching her green eyes darken when he smoothed his hands across her collarbone. He felt a shiver chase through her as he pushed the shirt over her slender shoulders. Rocking back on his heels, he lowered his gaze to her chest and watched the firelight dance over her exposed skin.

"Oh, Becky," he said on a shuddery sigh. "What have you been hiding from me?" Unable to resist, he leaned

*forward and pressed his lips in the shadowed valley be-
tween her breasts, savoring the sweet innocence of her
flesh, the scent of her. He heard, as well as felt, her sharp
intake of breath...then the slow relaxing of her body toward him. Slipping his arms around her, he unhooked her
bra and freed her breasts, baring her to the waist. The
color of rich cream, her firm mounds quivered in the cool
night air as if begging for his touch. Reverently he took
them in his hands, testing their weight, then stroked his
thumbs over her nipples, watching them bud. Hungry for
the taste of her, he dipped his head over first one, then
the other, suckling gently.*

*He heard her gasp of surprise as he raked his tongue
over the knotted flesh, felt the vibration against his
lips...then her hands were in his hair, drawing his face
closer to her.*

*He would take things slow, he promised himself as he
felt his blood heat. He'd teach her what she seemed so
hell-bent on learning, prove to her that he was the only
man for her. He stroked her flesh, smoothing his palms
over her back, letting her grow accustomed to his touch,
while he whispered words of praise and adulation in her
ear.*

*Guiding her down to the bedroll, he stripped her of her
jeans and boots, then removed his own, before stretching
out beside her. Smoothing his fingertips from the hollow
of her throat, down through the valley between her
breasts, he finally reached the rise of her feminine mound.
He closed his hand over her nest as he dipped his face
over hers, covering her mouth with his. He teased her lips
apart with his tongue, then dove deep inside. Her hands
tightened in his hair and her groan of pleasure vibrated
against his lips, his chest. Slowly he began to stroke her,*

showing her what all her body was capable of feeling, of experiencing.

Her response both surprised and pleased him, her readiness obvious in the increased pressure of her body against his. He rolled on top of her, mounting her, his need for her as strong as hers for him. With his breath burning in his lungs, he pressed his arousal against her. Tight. Oh, but she was tight. He pressed harder, heard her whimper, and eased back, soothing her with kisses on her eyes, her throat, her cheeks. "It's okay, Becky," he murmured. "We don't have to do this."

When he started to roll away, she wrapped her arms around him, stopping him. "No, please, Woody," she whispered. "I want this. You."

With a groan, he closed his mouth over hers and...

Forrest sat up in bed, his hands fisted in the cool satin sheets, his chest heaving. He looked wildly around the room, expecting to find the campfire and Becky...and slowly came to the realization that he was in the guest room alone.

But it was so real, his mind warred. He dragged the back of his hand across his mouth, sure that he could still taste her.

A dream, he told himself. It was all a dream. There was no way that he'd ever touch Becky in that way, nor would she let him.

Not when she was promised to another man.

With a growl, he swung his legs over the side of the bed. He was going to get that black book of his and by God he was going to find himself a wife, if it was the last thing he ever did.

Though embarrassed to do so, Becky relayed the previous night's happenings to Miss Manie when the woman appeared unannounced at the Rusty Corral shortly after Becky's return from the coyote hunt. She was sure that Miss Manie would be shocked when she heard that Becky had come close to baring herself to Woody. Instead she hooted at the ceiling and clapped her hands with glee.

"Now you've got him going," she chortled, her wattles quivering with her excitement. "Oh, what I would've given to see the look on that boy's face."

Even thinking about the look on Woody's face made Becky's face heat and her insides go all soft and warm.

Miss Manie just laughed at the sudden rise in color on Becky's cheeks and leaned to give her knee a comforting pat. "You're doing just fine. Better than fine, in fact." She shifted to look around Becky, pulling her glasses down her nose as she peered at the kitchen door. "Are you expecting company?"

Becky twisted around just as a shiny black coupe pulled to a stop outside. She jumped to her feet. "Mrs. C," she cried, charging for the door. She pushed through it, clearing the steps in one leap, and ran straight into Kathleen Cunningham's waiting arms. She wrapped her arms tightly around the older woman's neck and clung. "Oh, I'm so glad to see you," she cried.

Laughing, Kathleen gave her a tight squeeze, then pushed her to arm's length so that she could see her. "It's good to see you, too. And I certainly like this welcome better than the one I received from Forrest."

"You've seen him?" Becky asked, struggling to keep her smile in place.

"Yes, I certainly have. The old grump," she complained, then laughed again. She looped an arm around Becky's waist and walked with her back to the house. "When I left, he was sleeping. I certainly hope the nap improves his disposition."

GET A FREE TEDDY BEAR...

You'll love this plush, cuddly Teddy Bear, an adorable accessory for your dressing table, bookcase or desk. Measuring 5 ½" tall, he's soft and brown and has a bright red ribbon around his neck – he's completely captivating! And he's yours *absolutely free*, when you accept this no-risk offer!

AND TWO FREE BOOKS!

Here's a chance to get **two free Silhouette Desire® novels** from the Silhouette Reader Service™ **absolutely free!**

There's no catch. You're under no obligation to buy anything. We charge nothing – ZERO – for your first shipment. And you don't have to make any minimum number of purchases – not even one!

Find out for yourself why thousands of readers enjoy receiving books by mail from the Silhouette Reader Service™. They like the **convenience of home delivery**...they like getting the best new novels months before they're available in bookstores...and they love our **discount prices!**

Try us and see! Return this card promptly. We'll send your free books and a free Teddy Bear, under the terms explained on the back. We hope you'll want to remain with the reader service – but the choice is always yours!

326 SDL CTKQ   **225 SDL CTKK**
(S-D-10/99)

Name: _____

(PLEASE PRINT)

Address: _____ Apt.#: _____

City: _____ State/Prov.: _____ Postal Zip/Code: _____

Offer limited to one per household and not valid to current Silhouette Desire® subscribers.
All orders subject to approval. © 1998 HARLEQUIN ENTERPRISES LTD.
® and ™ are trademarks owned by Harlequin Books S.A. used under license.   **PRINTED IN U.S.A.**

NO OBLIGATION TO BUY!

The Silhouette Reader Service™ — Here's how it works:

Accepting your 2 free books and gift places you under no obligation to buy anything. You may keep the books and gift and return the shipping statement marked "cancel." If you do not cancel, about a month later we'll send you 6 additional novels and bill you just $3.12 each in the U.S., or $3.49 each in Canada, plus 25¢ delivery per book and applicable taxes if any.* That's the complete price and — compared to the cover price of $3.75 in the U.S. and $4.25 in Canada — it's quite a bargain! You may cancel at any time, but if you choose to continue, every month we'll send you 6 more books, which you may either purchase at the discount price or return to us and cancel your subscription.

*Terms and prices subject to change without notice. Sales tax applicable in N.Y. Canadian residents will be charged applicable provincial taxes and GST.

Suspecting that she might be at least partially responsible for Woody's bad mood, Becky quickly changed the
subject. "I didn't know you were coming for a visit."

"Sterling's reception is tonight. I wouldn't miss it for
the world."

Becky opened the door for Mrs. C, then followed her
through, nearly bumping into the woman when she
stopped short.

"Manie Riley!" Kathleen cried. "What are you doing
way out here in the country?"

Manie fussed with the hem of her dress, settling it over
her knees. "I'm not so old that I can't drive myself
around, you know."

"From what I hear," Kathleen said, giving her a sly
look, "you're not too old to do a *lot* of things."

Manie adjusted her glasses, all but preening. "I like to
think I've got a few surprises up my sleeve, yet."

Laughing, Kathleen gave her a quick hug. "More than
a few, I'll bet." She glanced over at Becky who still hov-
ered near the door. "And unless my sources are wrong,
someone else is full of surprises, too."

Dang you, Woody, Becky cursed silently. *Why'd you
have to go and tell your mother for?* She shot a desperate
look Miss Manie's way, but the woman just looked right
back, her expression blank, offering no help. "Well,"
Becky began uneasily as she crossed to the table, "I can
explain all that."

"I should hope you can," Kathleen replied with an
offended sniff as she dropped down a chair. "After all,
you're like a daughter to me. I would've thought I'd have
heard about your engagement from you, instead of having
to hear it secondhand from Forrest."

Becky sank onto the chair, wishing that she could sink
all the way through the floor. Lying to Woody was one

thing, but lying to his mother was a whole different matter. The fact was, she couldn't. "I'm not engaged," she mumbled miserably.

Kathleen's eyes widened in surprise. "What! But Forrest said—"

"He thinks I am, but it's all a big fat lie."

"A lie?" Kathleen repeated. She glanced at Manie, then back to Becky. "But why?"

Unable to meet the woman's gaze, Becky ran her thumbnail along a scar on the table's surface. "It's kind of a long story, but the short of it is, Woody asked me to marry him and I told him I couldn't because I was already engaged."

"Forrest asked you to marry him and you refused?" Kathleen sank back in her chair, pressing a hand over her heart. "I don't believe this."

"Believe it," Becky muttered, "'cause it's the gospel truth. Only Woody didn't really ask me out-and-out, he made it sound like he was doing me a favor by offering to marry me, as if I was a charity case or something. That's why I made up the fiancé."

Kathleen stared for a long moment. "When did all of this happen?"

"About a week ago." Becky ducked her head in shame. "I thought if I made him jealous it might force his hand. You know, make him put up a fight for me."

Miss Manie huffed a breath. "Now that's a teewydie if I ever heard one." She turned to Kathleen. "*I'm* the one who encouraged Rebecca to string the boy along, so if you're gonna be mad at someone, make it me."

"Mad?" Kathleen repeated. "I'm not mad. I'm furious!"

Becky braced her hands against the table and wearily pushed herself to her feet. "I'm sorry if I've disappointed you, Mrs. C. I'll call Woody right now and tell him the truth."

Kathleen caught Becky by the arm and jerked her back down in her chair. "No you won't!"

Becky stared at her, her forehead wrinkled in confusion. "I won't?"

"No, you most certainly will not!" Kathleen pressed her lips together and tapped her manicured nails against the top of the scarred table. "If I could get my hands on that son of mine right now," she muttered, "I'd wring his neck."

"Why?" Becky asked in surprise. "Woody didn't do anything wrong. I'm the one who lied."

"A small indiscretion when compared to his thoughtless behavior." Her frown deepened. "Treats his livestock with more care than he does a woman. Just like his father."

"What?" Becky asked, watching as Mrs. C rose to pace the small kitchen, her brow furrowed.

"Newt was the same way. Not that he didn't love me. He just didn't think to show it. But I certainly took care of that." She stopped suddenly and turned to look at Becky. "You're going to Sterling's post-wedding reception, aren't you?"

Becky shook her head. "No, I don't think so."

"And why not?"

Becky snorted. "You know Sterling. He's going all out. Black tie, the invitation said." She gave the collar of her shirt a tug. "I don't wear ties, black or any other color, for that matter."

"Get your purse," Kathleen ordered.

"What?"

"Get your purse. We're going shopping." She whipped around to Manie. "Are you coming with us?"

Sighing heavily, Manie pressed her knuckles against the table and pushed herself to her feet. "My bunions will never forgive me, but, yeah, I'm coming. It'll probably take the both of us to get this girl into a dress."

Forrest stood alone, sipping champagne from a crystal flute while watching couples glide by on the portable dance floor set up on the grounds of the Oasis, Sterling Churchill's private estate. The music was slow and seductive.

Though he hated wearing a monkey suit and attending events that required one, he'd made the sacrifice for Sterling's sake. Of course, the fact that he knew there would be a covey of available females on hand for him to check out as possible wife candidates might have tipped the scales a bit in favor of his attending.

He straightened as a blond danced by, held in the arms of one of Royal's bankers. Who is she? he wondered. The smile she offered Forrest was full of promise, and the finger she lifted from the banker's back, beckoning him to cut in on their dance, a bold move.

He forced a polite smile in return, but shook his head, then tossed back the last of his champagne. Too tall, he told himself. And too friendly. A woman who flirted with one man while dancing with another couldn't be trusted.

"Sterling sure knows how to throw a party."

Forrest turned to find Hank standing behind him, watching the dancers, too, his arms folded across his chest.

"If you go for froufrou," Forrest said, frowning. He lifted his nose and sniffed. "Smells like a damn funeral parlor. Where do you suppose he found so many fresh flowers this time of year?"

Hank chuckled. "Had 'em flown in from Hawaii. Used my jet."

"Why didn't he use his own plane?"

Hank nodded toward a line of buffet tables, which offered everything from caviar to bite-size lobster quiche. "His was busy hauling those ice sculptures and seafood delicacies from New Orleans." He chuckled. "He was about to have a coronary this morning, thinking they weren't going to make it here on time."

Forrest shook his head. "He'd have been better off throwing a steer over an open fire and tapping a keg."

Hank laughed and moved to clap a hand over his friend's shoulder. "That's what I like most about you, Forrest. You're a paradox. Beer taste and a champagne pocketbook."

"Just don't see what all the fuss is about," Forrest grumbled. "He got married at the courthouse, without telling a soul. Why the hell does he want to throw a reception now?"

Hank dropped his hand from Forrest's shoulder with a weighty sigh. "If you have to ask, then you're in worse shape than I first thought."

Forrest's scowl deepened. "And what's that supposed to mean?"

Hank folded his arms across his chest and turned his gaze back to the dance floor. "Women need certain things. Romance. Maybe even a little validation."

Forrest snorted. "A ring through a man's nose ought to be validation enough."

Hank shot him a look, then turned his gaze back to the dance floor. "You haven't found yourself a wife, yet, have you?"

"Not exactly."

"And how do you 'not exactly' find a wife?"

Forrest plucked a fresh glass of champagne from the tray of a white-coated waiter passing by, and replaced it with his empty one. He tossed back half the glass's contents before muttering, "Should've never mentioned to you and Sterling that I was looking for one."

His gaze set on the far side of the dance floor, a slow smile spread across Hank's face. "Well, would you look at that."

"What?" Forrest asked, then followed the line of Hank's gaze to where a woman stood, her back to them, talking to Sterling. Her dress was the color of midnight, so dark a blue it was almost black, but when she moved, metallic threads woven discreetly through the fabric caught the light and glittered like fool's gold. Though the dress was plain compared to most of the ladies' beads and spangles, Forrest quickly decided that, if it came to a vote, the simpler dress would win hands down.

"Who is she?" he asked, craning his neck for a better look.

At that moment, Sterling caught the woman's hand and tugged her out onto the dance floor. As they passed under one of the torches positioned strategically around its edge, the woman turned to laugh at something Sterling said and Forrest got a look at her face.

His fingers tightened on the stem of crystal. "Becky?" he choked out.

"In the flesh," Hank confirmed, his smile broadening.

As they both watched, Sterling twirled Becky in a fast, dizzying circle. The hem of her calf-length dress billowed out, exposing an expanse of bare leg, before he pulled her, laughing, into his arms. Forrest's stomach knotted as he watched her melt against Sterling's chest. He strained to keep the two in sight as they quickly blended in with the other dancers.

"Becky always could outdance any woman in Royal," Hank offered conversationally. "She's so light on her feet, she can make even an old gimp-legged pilot like me look like Fred Astaire."

"Dream on," Forrest muttered, his mood turning cantankerous as he watched the two deftly navigate the floor. "Nobody's that good."

"Becky is," Hank said with conviction. "Why, I remember dancing with her at a barbecue on the Golden Steer not long after I returned home from the service." He chuckled, rubbing at the leg that still gave him fits on occasion. "I could barely walk, much less cut a rug on the dance floor. I was feeling more than a little sorry for myself and hell-bent on drinking myself into a blind stupor when the band leader announced a lady's choice. Out of all the men there, Becky chose me." He shook his head in wonder as he remembered the night. "Holding a pretty little thing like her, feeling all those feminine curves and knowing full well that she could have chosen any one of the young bucks there as her partner...well, it gave me a new lease on life, that's what it did."

Forrest watched Becky pop a kiss on Sterling's cheek, and felt his blood begin to boil. "Shameless," he said in disgust, letting his gaze drop to the swell of breasts that the dress's heart-shaped neckline revealed. "And her an engaged woman."

"She ain't married, yet," Hank reminded him drolly. "Until all the 'I do's' have been said and the names entered legally on a marriage license, I figure a woman is still fair game." He turned and clapped a hand on Forrest's shoulder again. "You know, this music is giving me an itch. Think I'll find that wife of mine, and give her a turn on the dance floor." He gave Forrest's shoulder a squeeze, then walked off, whistling under his breath.

His gaze still riveted on the couple, Forrest sucked in a raw breath as he watched Sterling's hand slide down low on Becky's waist. Holding one hand high above her head, Sterling gave her a small push and spun her beneath their uplifted arms, then gathered her close again and waltzed away.

"Show off," Forrest muttered darkly. Friend or not, at the moment, he'd like nothing better than to put a fist through Sterling's face.

Then, he remembered Hank's comment. Fair game, he'd said. Forrest tossed the champagne glass aside, gave his slacks a determined hitch at the waist, and headed for the dance floor.

As far as he was concerned, hunting season had just opened.

Six

Forrest stalked across the dance floor, roughly shouldering his way past the dancing couples who blocked his way without a care for the surprised and angry looks he drew. When he caught up with Sterling and Becky, he gave Sterling's back a sharp jab that brought the man up short.

"What the—"

But before Sterling could finish the expletive, Forrest was unwinding Becky's arm from around his neck and planting it firmly on his own shoulder.

"Hey!" Sterling cried as Forrest forced himself between the two. "That's my dance partner."

"Was," Forrest tossed over his shoulder. "I'm cuttin' in." He turned to look down at Becky, his dark scowl daring her to disagree. "Unless you have a problem with that?"

She slipped her hand around his neck and grinned up

at him. "Nope. In fact, I was hoping I'd have an opportunity to talk to you tonight."

"Well, I'm needing to talk to you, too." He danced her away from her former partner. "About this fiancé of yours," he began.

She tossed back her head and laughed. "Isn't that funny? That's exactly what I wanted to talk to you about."

"It is?" he asked in surprise, though he was sure that what she wanted to discuss would be poles apart from what he had to say.

"Yeah. I've got a few more questions I'd like to ask."

He bit back a groan, remembering the questions she'd posed the night before. "No way."

She angled her head in warning. "You lost the bet, remember?"

As if he needed the reminder, he thought glumly. "What kind of questions?" he asked, his voice heavy with dread.

"Dancing for starters." She glanced around to see if any one was listening to their conversation, then eased closer, lifting her face to press her mouth near his ear. "I've heard that dancing is a whole lot like making love," she whispered. "Is it true?"

He jerked his head from hers as if she'd scalded him, then quickly steered her around a slower moving couple before he plowed a path right up the unsuspecting couple's backs. "Where do you get these damn fool ideas?" he growled. "Dancing's, dancing. Period."

She looked up at him, her green eyes wide with innocence. "Oh, but I can see how the two would be similar," she insisted. "Just think about it, Woody. The rhythm, the intimacy, the moves."

Even as she made the comparison, her breasts brushed

seductively against his chest. He stumbled a step at the contact, but quickly recovered. "Sorry," he mumbled.

She smiled guilelessly up at him. "That's okay. Anyway," she said and, to his regret, returned to the subject with the instincts of a homing pigeon, "I remember reading once that, in more primitive societies, dancing is a part of the mating ritual, so there might be some truth in the claim."

He snorted and shifted his hand on her back...but tensed when his hand met bare skin. He stole a glance over her shoulder and saw that her dress had a diamond-shaped cutout across the middle of her spine, one he knew would reveal a bra—if she was wearing one. Rearing his head back, he frowned down at her. "What the hell kind of dress is this, anyway?"

She lifted a shoulder and smiled shyly. "A new one. Like it?"

He scowled and cupped the back of her neck, forcing her head beneath his chin so that she couldn't see the lie in his eyes when he told it. "It's okay, I guess, though they were awful stingy with the fabric."

She squirmed, trying to break free. "Woody," she cried, her voice muffled by the front of his shirt, "you're smothering me."

"Sorry," he mumbled and loosened his hold on her.

She huffed a breath, frowning at him, then turned her cheek to his chest. They danced their way around the perimeter a couple of times without any more questions being asked, and gradually Forrest began to relax. Though he'd danced with Becky a thousand times or more over the years, he couldn't remember ever holding her this close before. Most of their dancing had been of the line variety, where they stood side by side, with very little touching and a whole lot of stomping going on.

He was surprised to discover how small she felt, how delicate...and how womanly. With his knee wedged between her thighs and his groin pressed against her abdomen, guiding her in the Western waltz, he had to admit she was right. Dancing was a whole lot like making love. Their hips moved in unison, brushing lightly with each forward step, then retreating only to meet again, like one lover teasing another.

Unconsciously he began to stroke his thumb along the flesh bared in the diamond-cutout on her dress. He felt a sigh move through her, then the barest touch of her fingertips against the curve of his ear.

"I can feel your heart beating," she said softly.

He dipped his chin, but could see nothing but the top of her head. "You can?"

"Yeah. Can you feel mine?"

He felt it, as well of the swell of breasts that pressed against his chest. "Y-yeah," he stammered, suddenly finding it difficult to breathe, much less talk.

Her fingertips traced the shell of his ear and a tremor rocked through him strong enough that he was sure it was being measured on a Richter scale in California by some seismologist.

"I think I understand now why so many religious groups are opposed to dancing," she said, thoughtfully.

"And why's that?"

She lifted her face from his chest to look up at him, her eyes wide with wonder at her newly found discovery. "Because it *is* a whole lot like making love."

Forrest swallowed hard as he stared into her eyes. Innocent, yet gleaming with something that looked dangerously close to lust. He knew he was going to have to put a stop to this conversation before he embarrassed himself...or her...or both of them.

Before he could, though, she rested her cheek on his chest again with a sigh.

"You know what, Woody?" she murmured softly.

"What?"

"I think I'm going to like sex."

He stumbled again, mumbled a quick, "Sorry," then moved on, his heart pounding against the wall of his chest like a herd of wild horses on the run. He gave himself a moment to compose himself before he asked, "And what makes you say that?"

"Well, I love to dance. Always have. So if dancing and sex are so similar, then I guess it would follow that I'm going to enjoy sex." She lifted her head to look up at him again. "Wouldn't it?"

Forrest just stared at her, unable to push a word past the lump that had wedged itself in his throat.

"Well, it does makes sense, doesn't it?" she asked uncertainly.

He stopped dead right there in the middle of the dance floor, then spun, dragging her by the hand behind him as he cut a quick exit from the dance floor.

"Woody!" she cried, all but running to keep up. "What are you doing?"

"I need something to drink," he muttered.

"Oh," she said, sounding disappointed, then brightened, hurrying after him. "You know, a drink does sound good. I worked up a powerful thirst on the dance floor."

Forrest stifled a groan. He'd worked up something powerful, too, while dancing, but it sure as hell wasn't a thirst…at least not for a drink. But a drink might be just what he needed, he told himself as he spied a swan-shaped fountain whose long beak released a steady stream of champagne. He let go of her hand long enough to grab two flutes from the linen-covered table, and stuck one under the swan's curved beak, filling it with champagne. He drained the glass while he waited for the other one to fill. He passed the second glass to Becky without looking at her and stuck his own glass back under, filling it again.

"Heavens, Woody," she said, watching him gulp champagne. "I didn't think you liked champagne."

"Don't," he mumbled, and filled the glass a third time. "But I don't see a keg anywhere around, do you?"

She glanced across the beautifully landscaped grounds, truly an oasis when compared to the rest of West Texas's barren landscape, but even more so now with all the twinkling lights and baskets of fresh flowers scattered everywhere. "No, but I could go up to the house. I'm sure Sterling's probably got a six-pack or two in the fridge. He usually does."

He turned to her, his mouth twisted in a scowl. "How the hell do you know what Sterling keeps in his refrigerator? Just exactly what have the two of you been up to all these years?"

Her eyes widened in surprise. "Sterling's one of my best friends," she said defensively, then frowned and stepped closer, peering closely into his eyes. "Are you drunk?"

"No, I'm not drunk," he groused and swung an arm out to keep her from drawing any closer. But the combination of the champagne he'd chugged and the wildly made gesture overbalanced him, and he grabbed for her to keep from pitching forward.

Becky staggered beneath the unexpected weight, but quickly wedged herself against his side and slid an arm around his waist to support him. "I think maybe you better sit down for a little while," she suggested a little shakily as she guided him toward a stone bench curved around the trunk of a tree.

"You'll sit with me, won't you, Becky?" he asked.

She sputtered a laugh at the little boy sound in the request. "Yeah, Woody. I'll sit with you."

She eased him down, and he laid his head back with a groan and closed his eyes. For a moment, she thought that he'd passed out, but then he dropped a hand onto the bench beside him and patted the smooth stone.

"Sit," he mumbled. "You promised."

Biting back a smile, she sank onto the bench beside him. She set her glass aside, folded her hands on her lap, looked up at the moon, down at the ground, tipped up the toes of her new heels to admire them, then glanced over at Woody…and had to fist her hands in her lap to keep from reaching out and smoothing back into place the lock of hair that had fallen over his forehead.

She inhaled a shuddery breath, then released it slowly so as not to disturb him. And she'd thought she liked him best when he was dressed in his work clothes. As she looked at him now in his starched, white, banded-collar shirt with its turquoise studs and smooth pleated front, she wondered how she could have ever thought such a ridiculous thing. Woody was built for a tux. With those wide shoulders of his, and muscled chest. She let her gaze drift down over the ribbed plane of his abdomen and to the paisley cummerbund, smiling because she knew that more than likely he'd worn it at his mother's insistence.

With a lustful sigh, she forced her gaze past by the swell beneath his slack's zipper, then down the length of muscled thigh, over the hump of his knee and stopped at the silver-tipped toes of his custom-made black eel boots. Yeah, she'd been wrong, all right. Woody was even more handsome all gussied up.

She leaned over to brush a sprig of grass from the leg

of his pants, but froze when she felt the weight of his hand on her hair.

"You've got the most beautiful hair," she heard him murmur.

She glanced over her shoulder, and nearly wilted at the heat she saw in his eyes. Slowly, she straightened, keeping her gaze on his.

"Thank you," she whispered.

His hand slipped beneath her hair and his fingers cupped the back of her neck.

"And the most beautiful eyes. Green," he said, angling her face to look deeply into them. "I never noticed how green they were before."

Embarrassed, Becky ducked her head. "Cat eyes, daddy always said."

He sat up, bringing his other hand to her chin and forcing it back up. "No. Not cat eyes," he said, his voice growing husky. "They're much too pretty to be compared to something as common as a cat." Thoughtfully, he stroked his thumb along the edge of her jaw. "An emerald," he said after a moment. "They're the color of an emerald. A rare and priceless emerald. I'm gonna buy you one to match them."

A shiver chased down her spine at the seductive pull of his voice. He edged closer and she caught the musky scent of his aftershave, the sweeter scent of champagne on his breath.

She felt the pressure of his hand on her neck as he drew her face toward his. "I dreamed about you today," he told her, his breath whispering across her lips. "And you were right. You do like sex."

She closed her eyes against the heat in his. He'd never touched her like this, talked to her in such a way—nor had any man, for that matter—and she wasn't sure how to respond. But then his lips grazed hers, and forming a reply became impossible, unimportant. Moist, she thought as a delicious shiver chased down her spine. Icy cool and burning hot at the same moment. She wondered how that could be.

"And you're good," he added, nuzzling his nose against her cheek. "As good as you are at dancing."

She shivered again, letting her head fall back as his lips slid over her jaw and down the smooth column of her throat. His hand followed his lips movement, then disappeared, only to reappear at her breast. She sucked in a startled breath at his touch.

"So soft," he murmured, molding his palm around her fullness. "All these years you've been hiding all this behind a man's shirt and I never knew."

He lifted his head, drawing back far enough to look into her eyes. "Damn, but I must've been blind," he whispered as if unable to believe he could have missed something so obvious. He continued to stare at her, his silver eyes full of wonder.

A couple passed by, laughing at some shared joke. He glanced their way, his eyes hardening at the interruption. He stood abruptly, catching her hand in his, and quickly ducked around the tree, dragging her behind him.

"Woody," she cried, glancing back toward the house where the celebration continued in full swing, "The party..."

"Too many people," he growled.

She stumbled to a stop, forcing him to a halt, too, as she stared up at him, her eyes widening in dismay. "We can't just leave without saying goodbye. That would be rude."

"We're not leaving. We're going to the barn." He gave her hand a tug and took off again, lengthening his stride.

She quickened her step, trying her best to keep up with him, but the unfamiliar heels made doing so difficult. She stumbled and the strap of one shoe slipped off her heel. She tugged hard on his hand. "Woody, wait!"

He stopped as she bent over to readjust her shoe. But before she could slip the stubborn strap back over her heel, he was scooping her up into his arms.

"Woody!" she cried, wrapping her arms around his neck and holding on. "What are you doing?"

"Carrying you."

"But my shoe," she cried, glancing over his shoulder at the shoe that lay abandoned on the carpet of grass.

"I'll buy you another pair. Hell, I'll buy you a damn shoe store!"

Stunned by the anger in his voice, she turned to stare at his shadowed profile. With the twinkling lights and glowing torches left behind, there was only moonlight to illuminate the determined set of his jaw, the angry glint in his eyes. Then they were passing through the barn's double doors and, for a moment, she could see nothing but inky blackness.

A horse shifted in his stall, making a whiffling sound as they passed, then there was only silence and the labored sound of Woody's breathing. He stopped in the center of the long alleyway and simply stood, his chest heaving, the muscles in his arms bulging beneath his jacket. Becky held her breath, staring at his profile as her eyes adjusted to the lack of light, unsure what to say or do.

Slowly he turned his face to hers. In the darkness, his features seemed sharper, his eyes darker, while his mouth was curved downward in the same frown it seemed he'd been wearing since she'd first told him of her engagement. Longing for the easy relationship they'd once shared, and wanting desperately to see one of the laughing smiles he'd once sent her way, she pressed a fingertip against his lips. She felt the warmth of his breath, the barely suppressed anger, then his hold on her was loosening, and she felt herself slipping. When she tightened her arms around his neck to keep from falling, he twisted her around, and held her against him as he slowly guided her body down the length of his.

Her feet touched the ground and she started to drop her hands, but he caught them in his and forced them back around his neck, holding them there as he looked down at her. "You're not getting married."

She widened her eyes in surprise at the anger in the command. "I'm not?"

"No," he growled. "And if you need convincing, then I'm prepared to change your mind right here and now."

"H-how?"

He inhaled deeply, as if struggling to get a grip on his temper. She could almost see the tension melt from him as he forced out the breath. As he did, his jaw softened, as did his tone. "Like this." With his gaze on hers, he opened his hands over hers. The strength was there, but there was a tenderness as well as he slid his palms slowly down the length of her arms. Gooseflesh popped up on her skin as he moved his hands on, smoothing them over her shoulders, down her back, until they settled low on her waist. He urged her hips toward his and their abdomens bumped gently, then welded together as heat burned against heat.

When Miss Manie had said that if she pushed hard enough, Woody would be forced to fight for her, Becky had envisioned him physically fighting another man for her hand. But as she looked at the raw need in his eyes and realized his intent she knew that *this* was what Miss Manie must have meant.

And it was one battle Becky was more than willing to let Woody win.

She watched his face draw nearer, the heat in his gaze bringing a flush of heat to her cheeks. "Oh my," she whispered, her breath coming out on a thready sigh. Then his lips were touching hers. Where his first kiss had been tentative, this one was anything but. He traced the shape of her mouth with his tongue, sending shivers chasing down her spine, then teased her lips apart and slipped inside, closing his mouth fully over hers.

A fire sparked to life low in her abdomen, and with each stroke of his tongue it blazed higher and hotter, until her breasts ached for the touch of his hands again. Desperate to ease the pang, she tightened her arms around his neck and pressed herself tightly against him. But the gentle chafing of his starched shirt on her tender breasts only made them throb all the more.

Moaning her frustration, she flattened her hands against his chest, trying to push away from him.

The pressure of her hands slowly registered in Forrest's lust-filled brain, and he lifted his head. Sure that she was going to demand that he stop, he met her gaze. The desire he saw there made him tighten his hands on her waist.

"What?" he said, his voice husky.

"Your shirt," she said, pressing a hand over her breast. "It's so stiff it's hurting me."

"I can fix that," he said quickly and immediately shrugged off his jacket. He tossed it aside and started to work on the turquoise studs that lined the front of his shirt. Once free of it, he tossed the shirt on top of his jacket.

"Better?" he asked, moving to take her in his arms again.

With her gaze fixed on the wall of his chest, she braced her hands there, transfixed by the warmth and play of

muscle beneath her palms. "Yeah," she said, then with a
sigh, laid her cheek between her splayed hands, feeling
the rhythmic beat of his heart. "Much better."

He wrapped his arms tightly around her and gently
rocked in rhythm with the muted music drifting through
the barn doors. His chest swelled at the feel of her body
pressed against his, his heart at the rightness of her being
in his arms. Perfect, he thought locking his arms around
her. He should have known all along.

He shifted slightly, slipping a knee between her thighs,
and rubbed his groin against her abdomen, mimicking the
posture of their earlier dance, then tipped her face up to
his. He looked deeply into her eyes, searching for any
sign of reluctance or hesitation. What he found was a need
that burned as hot as his own. *She doesn't love this fiancé
of hers,* he told himself. *If she did, she'd never be looking
at me this way, or allowing me to hold her so close.* Freed
by the assumption, he closed his mouth over hers.

He sipped at her lips, then drank deeply, greedily, moving his hands to frame her face, as if in doing so he could
somehow consume her. But kissing wasn't enough. He
wanted to touch her, see her…all of her.

Finding the button at the top of the diamond-cutout on
her back, he fumbled with it and was ready to rip it off
when it suddenly opened in his hand. With nothing to hold
it in place, the silk fabric slipped over her shoulders.
Breaking the kiss, he stepped back and eased the dress
farther down her arms, baring her breasts to his starving
gaze. They were just as he'd dreamt. Creamy smooth,
with dark rose-colored centers. As he stared, the nipples
budded into hard knots that trembled, seeming to beg for
his touch.

As he had in the dream, he lifted a hand and cupped
his palm over a breast, molding his fingers around its full

shape. At the same time, he lifted his gaze to hers. He could feel the frantic beating of her heart beneath his hand, could see the throbbing of her pulse in her throat, the heat in her glazed eyes. "I want to taste you," he whispered. Without waiting for her permission, he dipped his head over her breast, teasing with his tongue the distended nipple he'd exposed. He heard her soft mewl, felt the vibration of it against his lips. Sensing her acceptance, he opened his mouth fully over her and drew her in. Her fingers dug into his shoulders as she arched back, giving him easier access.

He moved from one breast to the other, alternately suckling and nipping, until she was all but sobbing his name. Slowly he withdrew, rubbing his thumbs over the moistness he'd left on her breasts. "I want to make love to you," he said, his voice raw with need.

"I—I know," she whispered brokenly. "I want that, too."

Glancing around, he worried for a moment at the lack of privacy the barn offered, wishing he had something better to offer her for her first time, then grabbed her hand and tugged her behind him as he stepped through the open doorway of the tack room. Turning, he pulled her into his arms again and pressed her back against the wall, crushing his mouth over hers. The pleasure of feeling her body molded against his drew a groan from deep within him.

Blinded to everything but this consuming need to touch her, to have her, he smoothed his hands over her hips and down her thighs, then brought them up, gathering the skirt of her dress at her waist. Nothing but a strip of lace with no more fabric than his handkerchief separated her from him. Anxious to rid her of that, as well, he slipped his thumbs behind the elastic and held his breath, sure that she would stop him before things went any farther. When she didn't, he released the breath on a sigh, and peeled the lace down, letting it drop to pool around her ankles.

"*Ahhh,* Becky," he groaned against her lips. He cupped his hands on her buttocks and squeezed, whispering her name again and again and again. "I won't hurt you," he promised as he slipped a hand between them. "I'd never hurt you." To prove it, he pressed tender kisses on her eyes, her cheeks, against the gentle curve of her ear as he began to stroke her and prepare her for what was to come.

"Woody," she gasped, arching against his probing fingers. "I—you— Oh, Woody," she cried helplessly.

"*Shhh.* It's okay," he soothed and shifted. Catching her low on her hips, he lifted her higher on his chest until her feet cleared the floor. "Hold on to me," he whispered. "And wrap your legs around my waist."

When she'd done as he instructed, he braced her back against the wall, and freed a hand to fumble with the zipper on his slacks. With both arms around her again, he lifted her higher. His breath was coming hard, his chest heaving as he fought for a control that was quickly slipping away. "It might hurt a little at first," he warned breathlessly. "But not for long. I promise."

He saw the uncertainty in her eyes, as well as the desire, but it was the trust he saw there that squeezed his heart. Slowly he lowered her, guiding her down to him. He felt her tense when their sexes first met, heard a low guttural groan and recognized it as his own. Perspiration beaded on his forehead, dampened his back, as he strained, fighting the need to bury himself in her.

Gently he arched his hips upward, easing inside her. She dropped her forehead against his on a muffled whimper, digging her fingers into his neck.

And then she began to move.

Dancing, he remembered her saying. Making love was like dancing. And it was. The sweetest, most beautiful dance he'd ever partnered. Her hips rose and fell against his, taking him deeper, then deeper still, while the rest of her body swayed against his—her breasts caressing his chest, her abdomen chafing against his groin, fanning the flames of his need higher.

His arm cramped and he braced it against the wall, lengthening the muscle, supporting her with only one arm while he allowed her to set the pace, the rhythm. He could feel the quickening of her breath against his face, the tightening of her feminine walls around his erection, and knew that heaven was just a step away.

Unable to hold back any longer, he pushed from the wall, held her tight against him and thrust hard, burying himself deeply inside her. She braced her hands at his shoulders, and threw back her head, arching against him as she cried out his name. Never in his life had the sound of his own name brought him so much pleasure. He held her against him, feeling every tremble, every beat of her pulse, as if it were his own.

Then he began to turn slowly, then faster, until he was spinning her in a dizzying circle.

She grabbed for him, wrapping her arms around his neck and holding on tight. "Woody!" she cried. "What are you doing?"

"Dancing." He laughed and spun faster. "Damn, if you weren't right. Making love *is* just like dancing."

Forrest picked up his shirt and shrugged it on. "We can marry on your birthday, if you want. Marrying so soon after breaking your engagement might raise a few brows, but nothing we can't handle." He opened his fly and started stuffing his shirttail inside his slacks. "I'll even go with you when you tell your fiancé you're not going to marry him." He stopped with one hand still inside his slacks when he saw the stricken look that came over Becky's face. "What?" he asked in concern.

Sitting fully dressed on a bale of hay across the alley-way from him, she dropped her chin, but not before he saw the glimmer of tears in her eyes. "Nothing," she murmured.

He quickly yanked up his zipper and crossed to hunker down in front of her. Bracing a hand on her knee, he tipped up her chin. "Doesn't look like nothing to me," he said softly, thumbing away a tear that leaked onto her cheek. "You're not sorry about what we did, are you?"

She wagged her head. "No. It's just that—"

"Forrest? You in there?"

They both jumped guiltily at the sound of Greg Hunt's voice. Slowly Forrest stood, placing himself between Becky and Greg, giving her the opportunity to compose herself. "Yeah. I'm here."

Greg Hunt stepped from the shadows and into the door-way. "Man, I've been looking all over the place for you!"

"Just wanted to get away from the noise for a while," Forrest replied.

Greg snorted a laugh as he stepped inside the barn. "Can't say that I blame you, but unfortunately your pres-ence is needed. Seems there's a problem with that foreign deal we've been trying to put together." He squinted up at the ceiling and the darkened light fixtures as he crossed to join them. "Why didn't you turn on some lights? Hell, I can't see a thing."

"Didn't want to disturb the animals."

Greg snorted again, then grinned when he saw Becky.

He leaned around Forrest to extend his hand to her. "I hear congratulations are in order."

She looked up at him in confusion as she accepted it. "What for?"

He laughed. "Your engagement, silly. Sterling was just telling me that you're getting married. Is it in the water or something?" He gave Forrest a poke in the arm. "If it is, I don't know about you, buddy, but I'm swearing off the stuff." He laughed again as he turned and headed back outside. "Hank's waiting for us in Sterling's office," he called over his shoulder. "Better put the hustle on it. He said it was important."

Forrest stared at Becky's face, watching the tears bud in her eyes again. "Don't," he said, his voice raw, sure that it was guilt at the mention of her engagement that drew them.

She caught her lower lip between her teeth and squeezed her hands into a fist in her lap. "Woody, I need to tell you something."

By the misery in her voice, Forrest suspected that the guilt was eating pretty deep.

"Hey! Are you coming, Forrest?"

Forrest snapped his head around at Greg's impatient call and frowned at the door and the darkness beyond. "Yeah, I'm coming," he yelled.

He dropped to his knee in front of Becky, covering her hands with his. "Wait for me. This shouldn't take long. As soon as I'm done, we'll talk. I promise. We can work this out. Everything'll be okay."

Seven

"I just received word that our foreign friend has boarded a jet for the United States."

Standing with his shoulder slouched against a paneled wall in his home office where the men from the Alpha team had gathered, Sterling straightened, his eyes sharpening with interest. "Alone?"

Hank tossed the fax onto the desk. "Far as we can tell."

"Let him come," Greg growled. "I'd like to go a round or two with that son of a bitch."

Reared back in the chair with his fingers templed over his chest, Hank replied thoughtfully, "You may get your chance." He rocked the chair forward and picked up the fax again. He studied it for a moment, then carefully folded it and slipped it into the inside pocket of his jacket. He shifted his gaze from one man to the next. "But our first concern is Blake and those kids."

Forrest scraped his hands through his hair, trying to shove back the thoughts of Becky that nagged at him. Though he'd wanted to stay with her, soothe away her worries, strip her of whatever guilt that might be eating at her, at the moment his presence was needed more here. There were lives at stake. Lives that he was responsible for. Blake. Anna's niece and nephew. With Prince Ivan in hot pursuit, Forrest knew that the danger surrounding Blake and the babies had increased tenfold. Anna had already lost her sister. It was up to him and the rest of the Alpha team to see that she didn't lose her niece and nephew, too. "Have you heard from Blake?"

"Not recently."

Greg rose to pace. "Do you think Ivan's picked up his trail?"

Hank shook his head. "I don't think so. That brother of yours is slick. He knows how to travel without being seen."

Forrest snorted. "Easy enough when you're traveling alone, but kind of hard when your luggage includes two little babies."

Greg whirled on him, his face flushed with fury. "If anybody can do it, Blake can."

Forrest held up his hands. "Hey. I'm on your side, remember?"

Hank stood, pushing back his chair. "Let's don't lose our heads now. We're too close to winning this thing."

"Well, what the hell are we supposed to do?" Greg cried in frustration. "Just sit here, twiddling our thumbs, and wait?"

Hank rounded the desk and placed a calming hand on Greg's shoulder. "That's exactly what we're going to do." He gave his friend's shoulder a reassuring squeeze. "But while we're twiddling, we're going to keep our eyes peeled and our ears tuned for any sign of trouble.'' He glanced around the room, meeting each man's gaze in turn. ''My guess is that Prince Ivan won't waste his time chasing Blake. It's Anna he wants. To get her, he'll have to go through us. And that means he'll have to come to Royal.''

Forrest strode across the lawn, searching among the remaining guests for a mane of red hair and a dress the color of midnight that shimmered like fool's gold when the light hit it just right. He made it all the way to the barn without finding either, then started working his way back. He tripped on something in the darkness, stopped and looked down, and realized it was Becky's shoe that he'd stumbled over.

He stooped and picked it up, chuckling to himself as he slipped it into the pocket of his tux's jacket. He gave the pocket a pat, then continued on his search. He scoured the grounds for half an hour before he finally had to admit that she was gone.

It's late, he reassured himself, when panic tried to slip in and grab him. He'd told her he'd only be a few minutes, but the meeting had taken more than an hour. She'd probably grown tired of waiting and gone home.

He stuffed his hands into the pockets of his slacks and headed for the line of uniformed valets, waiting by the driveway. It might be late, but he didn't care. He was going to the Rusty Corral and get this mess straightened out. He wasn't going to let whatever sense of duty Becky might feel toward her fiancé to force her into marrying a man she didn't love.

By, God, she was marrying *him!*

Becky climbed from her truck, then braced a hand against its side as she slipped off her one remaining shoe.

Feeling the swell of tears rising again, she fell back against the side of the truck and turned her face up to the star-filled sky.

How am I ever going to get myself out of this mess? she cried silently.

It had all seemed so innocent when Miss Manie had first laid out the plan. Make Woody jealous. Tease him a little. It was all a matter of forcing his hand, Miss Manie had said. She'd insisted that Becky just had to keep up the farce long enough for Woody to realize he loved her and was ready to put up a fight for her.

She dragged a hand across her cheek, swiping angrily at the unwanted tears. Not that she blamed Miss Manie for the mess she was in. Becky knew that she, herself, was the one who was responsible. She was the one who had told the lie. She was the one who had worked so hard to make Woody jealous. She was the one who had teased.

Oh, Miss Manie might have given her a little nudge of encouragement to keep the lie going and given her a few pointers on how to tease. And Woody's mother might have played a small part in the deception by helping her select a proper dress. But the lie itself was hers, and hers alone. The problem was that it had grown to the point where she wasn't sure how to unravel it. She knew she had to tell Woody the truth and was scared to death that, when she did, he might never forgive her.

So now here she was, alone, standing barefoot in the yard of the Rusty Corral, feeling a little like Cinderella must have felt after leaving the ball. And she probably looked a bit like her, too, she thought, glancing down at her dress. She caught the skirt of her dress, let the moon dance on the metallic threads, then let it drop. Yeah, she was Cinderella incarnate, all right, she thought with a self-deprecating laugh. All decked out in a new dress that she'd spent almost a month's wages on and with a broken down truck instead of a pumpkin for a royal carriage.

Remembering the shoe she still held, she lifted it, letting it dangle from one crooked finger. No glass slipper for this Cinderella, though, she thought wryly. Just a fancy black sling-back shoe, worthless to a woman who wore boots most of the time, and even more so since she'd lost its mate.

With a sigh, she pushed away from the truck and headed for the house, swinging the useless shoe at her side. At the back door, she paused, and looked over her shoulder one last time at the moon. A falling star streaked across the velvety sky. She closed her eyes and made a quick wish, praying that somehow Woody would find it in his heart to forgive her the lie. Without looking back, she opened the door and stepped inside.

"Hi, Beck."

She froze, her eyes going wide. "Shorty?" She glanced behind her and to the shadowed yard beyond. "I didn't know you were here," she said, turning back to her father. "Where's your truck?"

"Sold it."

Her eyebrows shot up, then slammed together over her nose as she narrowed a suspicious eye at him. "Sold it or lost it?"

Her father lifted a shoulder, but kept his gaze on the table and the toothpick he was shredding between his fingers. "Same thing," he muttered.

"No," she said, tossing her shoe onto the kitchen counter. "If you'd sold it, you'd have something to show for it. If you lost it on a bet," she said, her voice rising, "then you have nothing."

"No need to yell," he complained, tugging on his earlobe. "I can hear just fine."

"I'm gonna do more than yell, if I find out you've gambled something other than your truck."

He shifted uncomfortably in the chair and plucked a new toothpick from the holder to shred.

Becky watched his gnarled fingers pluck nervously at the toothpick and her blood slowly chilled. "What have you done?" she whispered.

Shorty kept his eyes on the splintered wood. "It was a sure thing," he muttered defensively. "The sweetest deal I've ever come across. I wouldn't've bought in, if I hadn't been sure it'd pay off big for us."

She took a hesitant step toward him. "What deal?"

He screwed his mouth to the side, but didn't reply.

"What deal?" she repeated, her voice rising.

"A stud," he said, scowling at the toothpick. "A handsome thing, too. Good conformation. Good bloodlines. Won plenty on the track."

"You bought him?"

He shook his head. "Too rich for my blood. Just bought into the syndication."

"How much?"

He caught his lower lip between his teeth and concentrated harder on shredding the toothpick.

"Shorty! How much?"

"The ranch."

The blood drained from her face. "You traded the ranch for a share in a horse?"

He tossed the toothpick to the table, and rose, pacing away. "It wasn't supposed to end up that way. The ranch was just collateral until the money started coming in." He jerked open the refrigerator door. "We were puttin' him up for stud. Ten grand a pop." He pulled out a can of beer, and ripped off the tab. "I'd've made my money back in a month's time, and bought back the deed, just as I'd planned, 'cept…"

"Except, what?"

"'Cept the damn horse shot nothing but blanks," he muttered, and lifted the beer to his lips.

The room seemed to shrink, the walls closing in tighter and tighter, until there was no air left to breathe. Becky bent double, hugging her arms around her middle. She was afraid that if she let go, she'd shatter and fly into a million pieces.

The ranch—her home—was gone. Traded for a share in a sterile stud.

She felt a hand on her shoulder, the touch as weak as the man who placed it there. "It'll be all right, Beck," he said gruffly. "We'll think of something. We always do."

"We!" she cried, flinging his arm from her as she jerked away from him. "Who is *we*? *I'm* the one who has worked this place and kept it together all these years, while *you*," she screamed, jabbing a finger at his chest, "chased your tail, gambling every cent I managed to save on some wild scheme."

He reached for her, but she backed away. "No. Don't touch me," she warned him, her voice trembling with rage. Then, choking on a sob, she whirled and ran from the house, letting the screen door slam shut on its rusty hinges behind her.

Forrest pulled up in front of Becky's house and rolled down his window, frowning at the dark windows. He started to open the door, then stopped and glanced at the clock on his dash.

Three in the morning.

Though tempted to go inside and crawl into bed with her, if for no other reason than to just cuddle, he dropped his hand from the door handle and reached for the ignition key. She would already be asleep, he told himself as he started his truck. No sense in waking her, not when he knew that she'd have to get up in a couple of hours to feed her stock. What he had to say would wait till morning. She wasn't going anywhere, and neither was he. A couple of hours either way wasn't going to change anything.

With a last longing look at the dark house, he turned the wheel and drove away.

"The tailor's here."

Forrest glanced up from his computer screen to look at his housekeeper who stood in the doorway of his office. "I didn't make an appointment with the tailor."

"No, but your mother did."

Forrest fell back against his chair with a groan. "Dammit, Marie. Why didn't you tell me before now, so I could cancel the dang thing?"

She lifted a shoulder, trying her best not to smile. "I didn't know about it either, till I answered the door and found him standing on the porch."

Wearily Forrest heaved himself from the chair. He was going to take care of this quickly, because he had another appointment to keep. This one with Becky. By noon, he'd have this whole fiancé mess straightened out and a ring on her finger. "Where is he?"

"In your bedroom." She stepped to the side to let him pass, then followed close on his heels. "He's already hauled in about a dozen bolts of fabric. There's one pink silk that looks really pretty."

Forrest shot her a dark look over his shoulder. Marie

always seemed to get some perverted sense of enjoyment out of watching he and his mother go head-to-head, and had for as long as he could remember.

She chuckled and continued to follow him. "Are you going to send him packing?"

"I would," he muttered irritably, "but it wouldn't do any good. Mom would just reschedule." He approached the wing that housed the master bedroom, his steps slowing with dread. "Might as well let him stick me full of pins and get it over with." Heaving a disgusted breath, he pushed open the bedroom's paneled double doors. Bolts of fabric in every shade of the rainbow draped his king-size bed. Beside it stood Chin-Liang, the tailor, his arms spread wide in welcome.

"Mr. Cunningham! So good to see you again."

Forrest crossed the spacious room in three long strides, unbuttoning his shirt. "Make it quick, Chin-Liang. I'm pressed for time."

Chin-Liang wagged a finger at Forrest. "You businessmen. Rush, rush, rush. All the time rushing. Not good for your health."

"There's nothing wrong with my health." Forrest ripped the shirt off and tossed it aside, then lifted his arms out to his sides, assuming the position, his expression that of a man facing a firing squad. "Just take your measurements, Chin-Liang. And I don't care what my mother told you, I only want white shirts."

Chin-Liang made a tsking sound with his tongue as he pulled a tape measure from around his neck. "White," he grumbled under his breath. "Always just white. How is Chin-Liang to make you look handsome, if you only choose white?"

The doorbell rang and Forrest glanced over his shoulder, frowning at Marie. "Get that, will you? And if it's somebody else my mother has sent out, tell 'em to get lost.''

Cackling gleefully, Marie scurried from the room.

Forrest turned back to meet his reflection in the cheval mirror Chin-Liang had dragged across the room and placed in front of him. He watched as the man moved around him, taking measurements, then hurriedly jotting them down.

''A new tux, your momma says,'' Chin-Liang said, and glanced up, grinning at Forrest. ''For your wedding, right?''

Forrest looked down at the wiry man, his brow furrowing. ''My mother told you I was getting married?''

Chin-Liang bobbed his head, grinning from ear to ear, as he wrapped the tape around Forrest's waist. ''Yes. Yes. She say Chin-Liang must sew quick, quick, because wedding is soon.''

Forrest lifted his gaze to frown at his reflection. How the hell did his mother know he and Becky were planning on getting married? Had Becky told her?

He felt his belt loosen, and glanced down as Chin-Liang began to unbutton the fly of his jeans. ''What the hell are you doing?'' he cried, batting the man's hands away.

''Must have good measurements,'' Chin-Liang replied and gave the denim a tug.

Forrest grabbed for the waist of his jeans, but Chin-Liang was quicker. Before Forrest could stop him, Chin-Liang had the jeans bunched around the tops of his boots and had a width of black fabric wrapped around his leg from thigh to ankle.

His cheeks flaming, Forrest set his jaw and glared at his reflection in the mirror. ''I'm gonna kill you, Mom,'' he mumbled under his breath. ''I swear I'm gonna kill you.'' He jumped as a sharp pain lanced his upper thigh.

"Dammit, Chin- Liang! What are you trying to do? Castrate me?"

Chin-Liang held up a straight pin, smiling sheepishly. "Sorry, Mr. Cunningham. Chin-Liang miss his aim."

"Becky's here, Forrest. Do you— Oh, my!''

Forrest jerked his gaze to the mirror to find Marie standing in the doorway behind him, her fingers pressed over her mouth, her eyes riveted on the backside of his boxer shorts. She sputtered a laugh and turned, ducking around Becky, who stood behind her, and disappeared down the hall. He could hear her wild gales of laughter until the kitchen door closed, cutting it off.

Frowning, he shifted his gaze on the glass to meet Becky's and his stomach clenched in dread when he saw her red-rimmed eyes. He twisted his head around to look at her. "Becky?" he asked in concern. "What's wrong?"

She drew in a deep breath, then took a step inside his room. "I came to give you my two-week notice." She pulled an envelope from her back pocket, and laid it on his dresser.

"Notice?" he said. "What notice?"

"I won't be able to work for the Golden Steer anymore." She drew in another deep breath, then added, "I'm leaving."

The knots in his stomach wound tighter. "Leaving? But last night—"

"Was a mistake," she said, before he could finish. "I'm sorry, Woody. Listen, I gotta go. I've got some packing to do." She spun on her heel and headed for the door. "You can pick up your stock whenever you want."

"Becky! Wait!" Forrest started after, swore when he nearly fell, hobbled by the jeans around his ankles. "Dammit, Becky, wait!" he yelled. He bent over and grabbed his jeans, jerking them back up over his hips as he shoved his way past the sputtering Chin-Liang.

He ran after Becky and caught up with her just as she was opening the front door. He slapped a palm against the thick wood, slamming the door shut before she could escape. "You're not going anywhere," he growled, "until you tell me what the hell is going on."

She stuffed her hands into her back pockets and backed up a step, her face pale. "I told you, already. I'm leaving."

"But we're getting married! Last night you said—"

"No, *you* said," she interrupted, cutting him off.

"So you're going to marry John Smythe—" he waved a frustrated hand "—or whatever the hell his name is?"

"Yeah," she said, lifting her chin. "I'm getting married."

He spun away, digging his fingers through his hair, his mind reeling. It wasn't true. It couldn't be true. He wouldn't *allow* it to be true. She'd made love with him last night. Him! Not this fantasy fiancé of hers. And Becky wasn't the kind of woman who would make love with one man, if her heart belonged to another.

He forced himself to take three long breaths before he turned back to face her. "You don't love him," he said, his voice rough with accusation. "I know you don't, otherwise you never would have made love with me."

Tears sprang to her eyes, but she lifted her chin higher, forcing them back. "You can think whatever you like, but the fact is, I'm leaving." She grabbed for the door and jerked it open, then darted through the opening, slamming it behind her.

Stunned, Forrest stared at the polished wood, then fell forward with a groan, planting both hands against the thick wood and burying his face in the crook of his arm.

She couldn't marry the guy. She just couldn't. He wouldn't let her. He brought a hand to his chest and fisted it over the ache where his heart used to be.

Dammit he loved her too much to just let her go.

Becky downshifted into second and took the turn onto the highway on two wheels. She dragged a wrist beneath her eye, and blinked hard, trying to see through the ocean of tears that blinded her.

It's better this way, she told herself as she fisted her hands tighter around the steering wheel. If Woody thought she was leaving Royal and the Rusty Corral because she was getting married, then he would never suspect the real reason behind her quick exodus.

She couldn't tell him the truth. She couldn't tell him that her father had gambled away their home. Her pride just couldn't take another beating.

She'd lived next door to Woody and his family most of her life, and though it embarrassed her to even think about it, she knew they were privy to every low point in her life. Those lean winters when she'd lived off beans and rice, and whatever wild game she could hunt. The overdrafts at the bank when Shorty had drained the ranch account. The patches on her jeans when there wasn't money enough to buy new ones.

In contrast, the Cunninghams lived up to the name of their ranch, the Golden Steer. She knew how wealthy they were. Heck! She could put ten houses the size of hers inside their home and still have room to spare.

It was bad enough to have next to nothing to offer a man in a marriage, but when a woman had nothing...

She choked on a sob, and pressed her hand against her lips to hold it inside. Nothing. She had nothing. No ranch. No home. Thanks to Shorty, in two weeks, she wouldn't even have a bed to sleep in. All she had left in the world was this old truck she was driving.

Even as the realization came, the truck backfired, lurched. The engine sputtered twice then died. Fighting to keep the truck on the road, Becky watched in wide-eyed horror as steam began to billow from beneath the hood. She steered the truck to the side of the road, pulled on the emergency brake, then dropped her head onto the steering wheel and gave in to the tears.

"Oh, Lord," she sobbed. "What am I going to do now?"

Forrest whistled to Rowdy, signaling the dog to turn the lead steer. Rowdy barked and snapped at the steer's nose, heading him toward the Rusty Corral's open gate, while Forrest pushed the rest of the herd on.

Forrest had originally planned for his wranglers to bring this small herd of steers over to the Rusty Corral and to the section of land he'd leased from Becky nearly a year ago. But after his conversation with Becky earlier that morning, he'd chosen to do it alone. Not that he needed an excuse to pay a visit to her, he assured himself. But he was going to have a talk with her, and she was going to listen.

She wasn't getting married. And if she was, it was going to be to Forrest Cunningham and *not* John Smythe.

He slapped his coiled lariat against his leg. "Get up there," he yelled, urging on a lagging steer. Reining his horse sharply, he cut off a brindle steer before he could break from the herd, then fell back to his position at drag. Once he was sure all the steers' noses were headed in the right direction, he glanced toward Becky's house in the distance. He frowned when he saw a car parked out front.

"Pick it up, Rowdy," he called, and spurred his horse

into a long trot, anxious to get the cattle settled in the pasture so that he could get back to the house and talk to Becky. Straining for a better look at the car, he saw a rental sticker on the rear bumper. With his heart pounding against his ribs, he cut his gaze to the house again just as Becky pushed open the front door.

She was juggling a pitcher and two glasses. She must have heard the cattle bawling, because she glanced up and her gaze met Forrest's. He watched the smile slowly melt off her face before she quickly turned away. It was then that Forrest noticed the man sitting in the wicker chair at the small table snugged into a corner on the porch. He watched, his stomach bottoming out, as Becky handed the man a glass, then draped a hand along his shoulders while she leaned to fill his glass with iced tea. The man looked up at her, smiled and said something.

Whatever he said, it must have been funny, because Becky tossed back her head and laughed. She sat down beside him, then pulled her chair closer to his. With her elbow propped on the table, she leaned closer to him, smiling, seemingly hanging on his every word.

Forrest wanted to race his horse across the distance that separated them, grab the man by the collar and bury his fist so deep in his face the guy would be chewing knuckles for a month.

But he couldn't. Not when there was only him and a dog herding sixty head of cattle down the lane. With a growl, he lifted the lariat again and slapped it hard against his leg. "Get up there," he yelled, pushing the cattle to a faster pace.

But he was coming back, he promised himself, just as soon as he closed the gate on the last steer. And when he returned…well, there sure as hell wouldn't be any laughing going on.

Becky watched the man drive away, a cloud of dust chasing his rental car down the lane. She shivered, and rubbed her hands up and down her arms. The guy was spooky. She couldn't figure out just exactly what it was about him that frightened her. His eyes, maybe? They definitely had a mean look in them, like a predator stalking his prey.

She shook off the uncomfortable feeling and turned for the barn and her chores. Though she'd been grateful when the man had stopped and offered her a ride home after her truck had broken down, she was relieved that he was finally gone. She'd been afraid there for a minute that she'd pushed her luck too far and that she was going to have get the shotgun she kept propped just inside the front door to fend off a sexual advance.

In retrospect, she could see how foolish it had been to use the stranger to put on a show for Woody, in hopes of leading Woody to believe that the man—Alfred, he'd said his name was—was her fiancé. But the setup had been too perfect to resist. She knew she didn't have to worry about Alfred ever denying her claim. He'd told her on the drive to the Rusty Corral that this was his first trip to Texas, and he was just passing through. He'd asked questions about Royal and the people who lived there, which she'd thought odd for a man who claimed the only purpose of his trip was to see firsthand Texas's varied topography.

She shrugged off the thoughts of the stranger and stepped inside the barn and to the chores that waited.

Ivan Striksky glanced in the rearview mirror of his rental car in time to see the young woman he'd rescued from the side of the road disappear inside a barn. For a moment, he considered turning back and giving the wench a nice long roll in the hay. Though a country bumpkin in his estimation and definitely beneath his royal status, the woman did have a certain charm. Her breasts for one, he thought, smiling lewdly.

His mouth curled into a sneer as he focused his attention on the road ahead. But he had more important matters to attend to. Anna von Overland. The princess had managed to escape…but not for long. He'd find her. And when he did…

Her chores complete, Becky slipped into the stall to check on the pregnant mare.

She moved along the horse's side, smoothing a hand over her swollen belly. Her time was close. Real close, if Becky was any judge. There'd probably be a new foal on the Rusty Corral before the week was out.

She felt a kick against her palm and smiled. "Feisty little fellow," she said to the mare, giving her a comforting pat. "I'll bet you'll be glad when this is over, huh, mama?" Taking a brush, she smoothed it down the mare's neck. "Won't be long now, though. And no need to worry. I'll be here with you. Everything'll be just fine."

"Is she in labor?"

Becky jumped, then forced her hand to resume its brushing as Woody stepped into the stall and closed the gate behind him. "Not yet. But she's close."

He moved to stand beside her, rubbing a hand along the mare's neck. "I put some steers on that section I leased from you last spring."

She kept her shoulder turned toward him, her gaze on her hand as she continued her grooming. "Yeah. I saw you. Shouldn't be a problem. I'll let the new owners know about the lease. I'm sure they'll honor it."

He whipped his head around to look at her. "New owners? You sold the Rusty Corral?"

She didn't want to answer, didn't want to have to admit to what Shorty had done. She didn't want to have to tell him that she could now be listed among the homeless. So she dodged the question, by saying, "They'll be taking over in about two weeks."

His hand dropped from the mare's neck, then he set his jaw and rammed his hands deeply into his pockets. "Who was that on the porch with you earlier? Your fiancé?"

"Yeah, that was him." The lie came easily to Becky. After weeks of lying, she was beginning to consider herself somewhat of a pro.

"I didn't see his car outside when I rode up. Where is he?"

"He left. Had some business to take care of in Pecos."

Infuriated by her indifference, he spun, kicking at the shavings on the stall floor, sending a cloud of dust into the air, then whirled on her. "Why are you doing this, Becky? You don't love him."

It was difficult, but she managed to keep her expression impassive and her tone light when she replied, "Says who?"

"I do," he growled. He grabbed her arm, jerked the brush from her hand and threw it down. Catching her by both arms, he spun her around to face him. "Admit it, you don't love him."

"I'll do no such thing," she cried, struggling to pull free. But he tightened his grip on her arms, his fingers digging into her skin.

"Then why did you make love with me, if you love another man?"

She lifted her chin defiantly. "For the experience. I told

you that I wanted you to teach me how to please a man."
She lifted a shoulder. "Now I know."

He dropped his hands from her so fast Becky stumbled
forward a step. He backed away from her, his eyes filled
with loathing, then he wheeled and stalked from the stall.
Becky listened to the sound of his footsteps, the creak of
leather as he swung up into his saddle, the click of hooves
against rock as he loped away.

Slowly she sank to the floor of the stall and buried her
face in her hands. Grief welled inside her, burning her
throat, stinging her eyes. And with it came a regret so
deep that it cut like a knife through her soul.

Eight

Forrest thought he'd been close to losing his mind when he'd returned from the mission in Europe, but his mental state then didn't hold a candle to the sense of madness that currently had him in its clutches.

When Becky had first told him about her fiancé, he'd been sure that she was lying…so sure that he'd insulted her with his offer to run a trace on the guy. But later, he'd been forced to admit that she really was engaged when he'd had proof of the guy's existence all but shoved in his face—the phone call, the roses. The one event, though, that had sent him careening over the edge had been Becky's request for him to teach her how to please a man so that she wouldn't embarrass herself when she made love with her fiancé the first time.

He snorted, dragging a finger beneath his nose. Love. If that was how a woman in love acted, he wanted no part of matrimony. He'd damn well live out his life alone with no wife to stand beside him and no kids to carry on the Cunningham name before he'd saddle himself with a woman who had no sense of loyalty, no respect for the vows she'd promised to take.

Even as the thought formed, he frowned, trying to place those attributes on Becky. For some reason they just wouldn't fit. In all the years he'd known her, he couldn't recall a time when she'd done anything that would make a person question her character. Becky Sullivan was a moral, law-abiding woman. Hell! He remembered a time when she'd found a twenty-dollar bill lying on the street, and hadn't rested until she'd found the person who'd dropped it. And, God knew, she could have used the money herself.

His frown deepened as he thought of all the work she'd done for the Golden Steer over the years when she could have just as easily accepted the charity his family had offered her and never lifted a finger in return. And as far as being loyal, wasn't the fact that she had stayed on at the Rusty Corral, taking care of her sorry excuse for a father, working her fingers to the bone to keep the place going, a sign of loyalty?

But she'd sold the Rusty Corral, he argued mentally, still having a hard time imagining Becky ever letting go of the place she'd worked so hard to keep.

Something's not right, he told himself with a shake of his head. There's more to this picture than meets the eye. He drove on a few miles, then braced a knee against the steering wheel and reached for his cell phone. He punched in a series of numbers, then brought the phone to his ear, glaring at the road ahead.

"Yeah," he said to the operator's offer of assistance. "Wichita. I need the number for John Smythe. That's spelled *S-m-y-t-h-e.*"

He waited for a response, impatiently thrumming his fingers against the steering wheel, then frowned when the operator came back on the line. "You're sure?" he asked uncertainly. "No, I don't have a street address," he replied to her question. He listened a moment, then mumbled a thanks and dropped the phone back onto its base on the truck's leather console.

No John Smythe listed in Wichita, Kansas. He pondered that a moment, then pressed the accelerator a little closer to the floor. Doesn't prove a thing, he told himself. Lots of folks had unlisted numbers.

And an unlisted number didn't resolve his questions as to why Becky would sell the Rusty Corral, either.

Still frowning, he drove down Royal's main street, headed for the Club. He glanced toward the line of cars parked along the street and suddenly stomped a foot on the brake. A horn blared behind him, and he quickly swung his truck into an empty parking space.

He shouldered open the door and jumped down, grabbing his hat before he pushed the door to behind him. Settling his hat on his head, he rounded the rear of his truck and backtracked to the car that had caught his attention. He stopped behind it, his gaze settling on the rear bumper and the name of the rental company displayed there. Moving quickly, he headed for the sidewalk and looked up and down, searching for the driver of the car. He spotted him half a block away.

"Hey!" he called, starting after him. "Hey, John! Wait up!" But the man kept walking.

Cursing under his breath, Forrest broke into a jog, ramming his hat farther down on his brow to keep the wind from stealing it. "Hey, John!" he yelled again. He caught up with the guy, and planted a hand on his shoulder and spun him around. "Didn't you hear me calling you?" he asked angrily.

The guy pursed his lips and lifted an arrogant chin, his eyes like daggers as he met Forrest's gaze. "I beg your pardon, sir," he said, imperiously. He lifted a manicured hand and pushed Forrest's hand from his shoulder. "I believe you have mistaken me for someone else." With that he turned and continued on his way, leaving Forrest behind, staring after him.

But Forrest wasn't mistaken. He *knew* that was the same man he'd seen sitting on Becky's front porch. The same one she'd claimed was her fiancé.

Forrest made the return trip to the Rusty Corral in under twenty minutes, burning up the miles with a heavy foot pressed against the accelerator. He braked to a gravel-spitting stop in front of the barn and shoved open his door. Once on the ground, he drew in a deep breath.

She'd lied to him. And now it was time to even the score. And he was going to love every minute of it.

He took another deep breath, forcing the tension from his shoulders, then hooked his thumbs loosely through his belt loops and whistled a cheery little tune as he strolled inside the barn.

In the midst of measuring out feed, Becky whipped her head around at the sound of his whistling. "What are you doing back here?" she asked irritably and dumped the scoop of feed into the bucket.

"Two things," he replied. "First, I want to apologize for how I acted earlier." At her surprised look, he rubbed a finger beneath his nose, and tried his best to look sheepish. "I guess you were right. Knowing you'd rather marry someone else other than me *did* put a dent in my ego."

She jerked her gaze from his and rammed the scoop

back into the bin, burying it deeply in the oats. "Apology accepted. What else?"

"Well, I had a thought," he said, and folded his arms across his chest. Smiling, he rocked back on his heels, feigning nonchalance. "Sort of a way to make up to you for the way I acted earlier." He paused a moment, taking a deep breath, then went on. "Since your fiancé's in town, and all, I figure that y'all will probably get around to doing the big one," he explained, using her term for the act. He had to work hard to keep from grinning at the horrified look that spread across her face.

She quickly ducked her head and dumped the scoop of oats into the bucket. "Probably," she muttered and lifted the bucket.

He calmly reached over and took it from her hands and set it aside. "And I know that you don't want to make a fool of yourself when you do," he said sympathetically. Smiling, he caught her hands in his and forced them to his shoulders. "So I thought I'd give you a few more pointers, just to show you there's no hard feelings."

"I—I think I've pretty well got everything down," she said, and tried to pull her hands from beneath his.

He tightened his grip and stepped closer, successfully trapping her between the wall of the barn and the equally unrelenting wall of his chest. "Oh, there's a few things you've yet to learn," he said, pleased when he felt the kick of her pulse beneath his hands. "Like kissing," he suggested as he dipped his head over hers. He ran his tongue along the seam of her lips, then sipped gently at them. "You're responsive," he murmured, withdrawing a little and licking the moisture from his lips as he stared at her sensuous mouth. "I can't argue that. But you need to be a bit more aggressive. A man likes it when a woman shows a more active interest in what's going on between them." He pressed his mouth over hers again, and murmured, "Give me some tongue. Tease me a little."

She pressed her lips firmly together and dug the heels of her hands into his shoulders, trying to push him away. He smiled against her mouth. "Come on, Becky," he urged silkily as he rubbed his chest seductively across her breasts. "Let me teach you all I know."

He felt the stab of her hardened nipples against his chest and the sudden trembling in her legs against his thigh, and knew he'd succeeded in arousing her. Shifting, he purposefully grazed her abdomen with his as he nuzzled his way across her cheek to her ear, then swept behind it to nip at the tender skin there.

She shivered, but continued to press against his shoulders, trying to push him away. "Woody, don't."

"Don't, what?" he asked as he slid his mouth down the smooth column of her throat.

"Don't do this to me."

"I'm not doing anything to you. I'm trying to get *you* to do something to me." He closed his mouth over a breast and nipped.

She gasped and dug her fingernails deeply into his shoulders. But she wasn't pushing away any longer. She was holding on.

"You like that?" he whispered, then nipped again. "Tell me how that feels, what it does to you."

She sucked in a trembling breath and closed her eyes, her head lolling back against the wall.

He dropped one of his hands from hers and slipped it between her legs. She bucked at the unexpected touch. "Can you feel it here?" he whispered, cupping her heat. "When I touch your breasts—" he paused to suckle the one nearest him "—do you feel it here, as well?" he asked, and gently squeezed his hand around her.

"Yes," she whispered, frantically nodding her head. "Yes, there."

He wedged his hips more firmly against hers. "Does it feel good?" he asked and nipped at her breasts again, this time succeeding in capturing a nipple beneath the fabric that covered them.

"Yes," she cried, arching against him.

He lifted his face to hers and increased the pressure of his hand. "Show me," he said, his voice growing husky. "Show me how good it feels."

Though Becky knew that making love with Woody again was a mistake, the memory of which would haunt the lonely nights ahead of her, on a sob, she wrapped her hands around his neck and crushed her mouth against his. She nipped his lips, as he had hers, then dived her tongue inside when they parted. With a wantonness she was only beginning to realize she possessed, she stroked his tongue, mating with it, matching the rhythm of his hand between her legs.

Crazed by the sensations that pulsed and built inside her, she pushed away from the wall. She wrapped her arms tighter around his neck and stretched to her toes, matching her body to the length of his. She ground her hips against his, wanting, needing, to be closer still.

"Make love to me, Woody," she gasped, dropping her hands to tug at his belt.

Forrest wasn't sure at what point he lost the need to get even to the more powerful urge to have her. But it was there, burning beneath his hands as he ripped open her shirt's snaps, baring her breasts to a hunger that gnawed low in his gut. He pressed hot kisses over the swelled mounds he'd exposed while she fumbled with the buttons that lined his fly. He suckled greedily while she struggled to free him, and when she took him in her hand…he knew there was no turning back.

The feel of her trembling fingers wrapped around him, the heat that rose between them, threatening to consume them both, blinded him to everything but the carnal pleasure she drew with each tremulous stroke.

Wanting to touch her as well, he quickly unfastened her jeans and worked his hand inside the denim. One brush of his fingers against the moist velvet folds and he knew touching wasn't going to be enough. He wanted inside her.

With a low, feral growl, he caught her up in his arms and closed his mouth over hers. Holding her high on his chest, he crossed to a stack of hay, his belt buckle slapping against his thigh. He set her down, his mouth still ravaging hers, and worked her jeans over her hips and down her legs. Wedging himself in the V formed by her spread knees, he drew her hips toward him. "Mine," he whispered, drawing back to meet her gaze. "You're mine."

He thrust forward, driving inside her, watching her eyes darken, then glaze. He squeezed his own eyes shut, groaning at the pleasure that shot through him in waves. He felt her hand on his cheek, then it was on his neck, pulling his face to hers. Her mouth met his, her breath warm against his lips, her taste as sweet as it was erotic…and he was lost.

Holding her hips between his hands, he arched against her again…and again…and again…and again. Driving himself against her until perspiration beaded both their bodies and they were both gasping and clinging to each other. He felt the pressure building inside him, the answering pulse of her feminine walls against his engorged shaft. A moan built that seemed to come from the deepest depths of his soul, and he dragged her from the hay and clutched her to his chest. She wrapped her legs around his waist and arched against him, crying out his name as he pumped his seed into her.

He stood, his back bowed, the muscles in his arms and legs trembling at the strain, until the tension eased from her body and she collapsed against his chest, burying her face in the curve of his neck.

He felt her hands wind around his neck, the moist warmth of her breath against his skin. And he knew that no matter what, he wasn't going to let her go. He wasn't going to lose her.

He pressed his lips against her hair as he eased her down on the bale of hay. "Becky," he whispered, placing his hands at her cheeks and turning her face up to his. "Marry me. Now. Right now."

He watched the color drain from her face, the passion from her eyes.

She brushed his hands away and slipped from the bale of hay and around him. "I can't." She grabbed her jeans and tugged them on.

Forrest watched her, shocked by her refusal. Then the anger came singing back. "Why the hell not? And don't give me that crap about being engaged." He jerked his own jeans back to his waist and began furiously to button them. "I *saw* your fiancé in town," he added scathingly. "John Smythe? Right? Funny. The guy didn't seem to recognize his own name when I called out to him."

Becky froze with her hands on the plackets of her shirt. Slowly she dropped them to her sides, knowing the game was over. "I'm not engaged," she murmured and dipped her chin in order to see to fit together the snaps that lined the front of her shirt.

"Now there's a surprise," he said sarcastically. He

shoved his belt through the last loop and hooked the buckle. "What I'd like to know is why you said you were in the first place."

Though a lie would have been easier to offer, this time Becky gave him the truth. "Because you hurt my feelings."

"What!" he cried, then demanded, "When?"

"The afternoon you first proposed." She combed her fingers through her hair, plucking at the pieces of hay that had somehow managed to embed themselves there.

Forrest remembered Hank's comment about how a woman didn't like being referred to as a spinster, and realized the old cuss had been right. "I didn't mean to offend you by referring to your spinster status," he said gruffly.

She shot him a dark look.

He rolled his eyes toward the ceiling and tossed his hands up in the air. "Hell. You know what I mean." At a loss as to what else he could say, he stuffed his hands into his pockets. "I just wanted to get married, was all," he muttered.

"You just wanted to get married," she repeated, her voice mocking, "and it didn't matter to who, just so long as you got yourself a wife. So you asked good ol' Becky, thinking you were doing me a big favor by doing so."

He scowled at the sarcasm in her voice. "That wasn't the way it was."

She folded her arms across her chest. "Oh, really? Then was it because all those other women turned you down? The ones you wined and dined after you got back from Europe?"

"I didn't ask anybody to marry me, except you," he cried indignantly.

"And why *did* you ask me?" she asked, her voice rising. "Did you wear yourself out romancing those other women so much that you didn't have any romance left to offer anyone else, so you turned to good old Becky, thinking I wouldn't require any?"

It took him a minute, but Forrest finally noticed the tears that gleamed in her eyes, and realized how deeply he'd hurt her with his backhanded proposal. "I'm sorry, Becky," he said, and meant it with all his heart. "It never occurred to me that you would want to be romanced."

She snorted a laugh that lacked even a glimmer of humor. "No, I'm sure it didn't." She turned and picked up the bucket he'd taken from her earlier. "You'll have to excuse me, Woody," she said tersely as she brushed past him. "I've got work to do."

He watched her stride angrily from the barn, and thought it best to let her go. At least for the moment. When Becky had a bee in her bonnet, Forrest had learned years ago to stay out of her way. Besides, he had some thinking to do. If Becky wanted to be romanced, then he'd romance her.

But first, he was going to have to find out how a man went about doing that.

The Royal Diner was the perfect place for heavy thinking. With the jukebox pumping out a popular country tune, and the scent of grease thick in the air, Forrest slid into his favorite booth and gave a nod at the coffeepot Anna held up in silent invitation from her position behind the counter.

She quickly crossed the room and upended a cup in front of him. "Have you heard anything from Blake?" she whispered.

Regretfully he shook his head. "Not recently. But we'll hear something soon, I'm sure."

Her brow furrowed with worry. "I hope so. I fear for his and the children's safety."

"Hey, Annie! Where's my fries?"

Forrest glanced in the direction of the counter and to the disgruntled customer who'd shouted the question, then back at Anna. "Has his drawers in a twist, doesn't he?"

She looked at Forrest in confusion, then laughed softly as the meaning behind his comment registered. "It seems you Texans have a phrase for every occasion."

"What does it take to get service in this joint, anyway?" the man complained loudly.

She heaved a weary sigh. "Excuse me, please," she said to Forrest. "If I don't serve Leon his fries soon, I'm afraid he might try to decide to stack the diner's furniture."

Forrest tossed back his head and laughed. "You're catching on," he said, lifting his cup in a salute. "You'll have the lingo down in no time."

He watched her hurry back to the counter, and noticed that a distant neighbor of his, Josie Walters, was among those huddled around the counter, listening to the news on the radio.

When the announcer issued a warning to those on the road to be on the alert for the possibility of wind gusts up to seventy miles per hour, Josie set aside her cup of coffee. As she turned from the counter, Forrest noticed the worry lines that plowed between her eyebrows, and wondered if it was the two hour drive that stretched between her and home that put the lines there. He watched as she stopped at a table to talk to Pete Mitchell, a drifter who did odd jobs around the county, and overheard her ask Pete if he would drop by her farm and make some repairs on her barn. Forrest saw Pete's hand slip to Josie's buttocks and started to rise, prepared to come to Josie's defense, then sat back down, chuckling softly when Josie picked up a cup of coffee and poured it across Pete's lap. Her face flushed with fury, Josie stormed for the door, fighting the wind as she pushed her way through it.

Forrest watched her fight the wind as she pushed her way through the diner's front door. Twenty-nine years old and a widow, he reflected sadly, and left with a farm to manage on her own. A hell of a situation for a woman to be caught in.

The thought drew an image of another woman who struggled alone to keep a place running, and the need to convince that woman to marry him.

He scrubbed his hands over his face, then slid down in the booth and stretched out his legs. He needed a break from this thinking business. His brain was plumb worn-out, and he still hadn't come up with a decent plan as to how to romance Becky. He turned his head to stare out the diner's window. Three days had passed since he'd last seen her and not one good idea had surfaced.

A boot hit his, snagging his attention, and he turned to find Hank standing beside his booth. Forrest sat up, drawing his legs underneath the table. He gestured toward the bench opposite him. "Have a seat."

"Don't mind if I do," Hank replied dryly as he slid into the booth. "Callie said you called."

"Yeah. I need some help."

Noticing the dark circles under his friend's eyes, Hank leaned forward in concern. "Are you sick?"

Forrest snorted. "I'm never sick."

Hank sagged back against the booth in relief, then frowned. "Well, you look like hell." The comment won a scowl from Forrest. "If you're not sick, then what's ailing you? Did the bottom fall out of the cattle market?

I've been gone a couple of days and I haven't been keeping a close watch on things.''

Forrest shook his head, as he drew his coffee cup between his hands. "No. At least, I don't think it has. I haven't been paying much attention to the market, either.''

Hank knitted his forehead in concern. If Forrest wasn't watching the market, then something was definitely wrong. "What's troubling you, then?''

Embarrassed to admit his problem, Forrest caught his upper lip between his teeth. He released it on a heavy sigh. "It's Becky,'' he finally admitted.

"Yeah, I heard what Shorty did. A crying shame, if you asked me.''

Forrest snapped his head up. "Shorty's in town?''

"Was. He's gone now.''

"What did he do?''

"You don't know?''

When Forrest shook his head, Hank leaned forward, bracing his forearms on the table. "Sold the ranch right out from under her. Or rather, gambled it out from under her,'' he amended, his voice heavy with disgust.

Forrest stared, unable to believe his ears. "How do you know about this?''

Hank lifted a shoulder, then sank back against the cushion, stretching out a leg and rubbing at the old scars there. "Heard it over in Del Rio. Seems Shorty bought a share in a sterile stud, using the ranch as collateral.'' He wagged his head regretfully. "Poor Becky.''

Stunned by the news, Forrest simply stared. "Why didn't she tell me? I'd have helped her.''

Hank lifted a shoulder. "You know Becky. She's got a lot of pride.''

Forrest swallowed hard, dropping his gaze to his coffee

cup. Yeah. He knew all about Becky's pride. Over the years, he'd been thrown up against it more times than he cared to think about. And she *had* told him she was leaving, he remembered guiltily. But when she'd given him the two weeks notice, he'd assumed it was because she was getting married.

And she'd let him go right on believing that, rather than swallow her pride and tell him what Shorty had done.

He was on his feet before Hank knew he'd even moved. "Who loaned Shorty the money?" he demanded angrily.

Hank looked up at him. "Some outfit over in New Mexico. The guy's name is Reed, I think. Don't recall hearing his first name."

Forrest grabbed his hat and rammed it on his head. "That's enough to go on. I'll find him."

"Hey, Forrest," Hank called after him. "Why'd you want me to meet you here?"

Forrest waved a dismissive hand in the air. Romancing Becky was no longer on his mind. Getting her farm back was. "It's not important."

Hank watched Forrest push through the door, then gave the bench opposite him a frustrated kick, muttering, "And here I left my new bride, who I haven't seen or slept with in three days, because she tells me Forrest called and asked me to meet him, sounding like he was caught in a life or death situation. And then the man has the gall to tell me whatever he wanted isn't important." He gave the bench another kick just for good measure, then pushed to his feet. "I wish he'd hurry up and get himself married," he muttered contrarily as he limped for the door. "He's puttin' a definite strain on my sex life."

Tracking down a deal that was made in a bar, written on a cocktail napkin and sealed with nothing but a handshake, took awhile. But Forrest would have chased the shadowy leads to the ends of the earth and back, if that's what it took to place the deed to the Rusty Corral back in Becky's hands.

As it turned out, he only had to go as far as Del Rio.

He arrived at dusk, via Sterling's plane, rented a car and headed for the Lowdown Saloon, a seedy watering hole where he'd learned Reed liked to conduct his business. Trucks of every description crowded the small lot he parked his rental in, and a neon sign blinked on and off promising cold beer on tap and topless waitresses.

After locking the car, Forrest pushed through the bar's tinted glass door and paused a moment to give his eyes time to adjust to the dimly lit interior. The Lowdown Saloon was like a hundred other beer joints he'd frequented over the years. A long bar stretched across one wall with about a dozen bar stools bolted to the floor in front of it. The mirror behind the bar offered a view of the remainder of the smoke-filled room. Tables for four were scattered around and booths lined two walls. A sign that read Fillies hung cockeyed on the wall and an arrow beneath pointed toward a short, dark hall with a pay phone at the end. A second sign, hanging below the first, read Studs, but someone had struck a line through the word and scrawled Geldings above it. Probably a woman who'd had a run of bad luck with men, he thought with a chuckle.

He braced his hands low on his hips and looked around, searching for a man who fit the description he'd been given. He'd covered only half the room when he felt a hand on his back. Before he could turn, a woman was winding herself around him like honeysuckle on a tree.

She looped an arm through the crook in his and smiled

up at him through a layer of mascara thick enough to tar a mile of bad road. "Hi, cowboy. Buy me a drink?"

He forced a smile in return as he carefully unwound her arm from his. "Sorry. I'm meeting someone."

She puckered her lips in a pout that he was sure she thought was sexy. "Not even one teensy weensy little drink?"

Hoping to get rid of her, he stuck a hand in his pocket and pulled out a money clip. He peeled off a fifty and handed it to her. "Here. Have one on me."

She caught the bill between two fingers and tucked it into her cleavage, a bottomless pit as far as he could tell as he watched the money disappear. Smiling up at him, she sidled closer, laying a hand on the middle of his chest, while she drilled a knee between his. She drew a circle on his shirtfront with a nail that she ought to be required to register. It was deadlier than any pistol he'd ever seen.

"I'd like to have one on you, all right" she said suggestively. "Maybe even two," she added with a wink.

Feeling the pressure of her knee rising higher on his thigh, Forrest cleared his throat and took a step back, separating himself from her. He strained to look over the top of a mountain of teased hair. "Excuse me," he said, and brushed past her. "I believe I just found my man."

He heard a huff of breath behind him, then her mutter something about why every good-looking man she met had to be gay.

He bit back a smile as he headed for the bar, wondering if she was the artist who'd redesigned the sign to the men's rest room.

"Whiskey and branch water," he said to the bartender.

"Be right with you" was the bartender's reply as he shook up a margarita.

Forrest turned his back to the bar, and reared back

against it, crossing his boots at the ankle. "Any action around here?" he said to no one in particular as he looked out over the room.

The man beside him shifted on his bar stool and lifted his glass. "Depends on what you're looking for," he replied and tossed back his drink.

"A game would be nice," Forrest said, turning back to the bar just as the bartender plopped a napkin in front of him and his drink on top of it. Forrest pulled out his money clip, peeled off a hundred dollar bill and dropped it on the scarred bar. He raked a thumb along the edge of the remaining bills, watching the man's reaction in the mirror. The guy all but drooled as he eyed the thick clip. "Though poker's my personal preference," Forrest added. He chuckled as he stuffed the wad of bills back into his pocket. "Course I promised my wife I wouldn't play anymore, after I dropped nearly a quarter mil last time we were in Vegas." He glanced over at the man. "You play?"

The guy lifted a shoulder. "Some." He angled his head to look at Forrest. "You from around here?"

Forrest took a sip of his drink. "Nah. I'm just in town for the night."

The man eyed him a moment longer, then stuck out his hand. "The name's Reed," he said.

Forrest accepted the hand, and smiled. "My friends call me Woody," he replied.

"Well, welcome to Del Rio, Woody." Reed thumped him on the back as he slid off his stool. "There's usually a game going on in the back," he said, as he gave his pants a hitch over a belly the size of a keg. "Follow me."

Smiling, Forrest fell in behind him. "Now if I start losing too much," he said to Reed's back, "you pack me off to home. Otherwise, my wife's liable to divorce me for sure this time.''

Reed turned and tossed an arm along Forrest's shoulders as he led him to the back room and what he must have considered a sure slaughter. ''Don't you worry none, boy. I'll take good care of you.''

Like taking candy from a baby, Forrest thought, smiling smugly. He tucked the deed into the inside pocket of his leather jacket, gave it a pat, then loped up the loading steps snugged up against Sterling's airplane's open door and ducked inside.

Nine

Boxes stood three deep in the gutted room and lined two walls, leaving only a narrow path that led to the kitchen beyond. Becky navigated the path carefully, straining to see over the top of the box she carried.

Her toe struck the leg of the kitchen table, and she sagged with relief as she eased her heavy load down onto the table's surface. Glancing around, she shook her arms, trying to get the blood flowing again, as she tried to decide what to do next.

She still had the freezer to defrost, but first she'd have to do something with the meat stored there. Making a mental note to call the community kitchen that fed the homeless, she moved her gaze on. The café curtains in the window were of no use to her and would be left with the house. And the stove wasn't worth what it would cost her to have it hauled off, so she'd leave it behind, as well.

She gnawed her thumbnail as she turned slowly. The

walls really needed a coat of paint, she thought with regret, but it was ridiculous to think about buying paint for the pleasure of the new owners, when she didn't even know where she, herself, was going to live.

Her gaze stopped at the hat rack by the back door and the tears she'd held at bay all morning swelled in her throat. Slowly she crossed the room and plucked a tattered Stetson from a peg. Woody had always left a hat at her house, along with a set of clothes and a pair of boots, never knowing when he might need a clean change of clothing. She turned the hat over and looked inside for the words she knew were printed there.

Like hell this hat is yours! This hat belongs to Forrest Cunningham.

The warning was pure Woody. Laughing through her tears, she pulled the hat to her face, inhaling deeply and drinking in his familiar scent—a combination of sweat and horses, blended with a pricey man's cologne. Turning the worn felt against her cheek, she crossed back to the table and sank down in a chair.

She set the hat, crown down, on her lap and smoothed her fingers along the brim as she looked around the room. Mercy, but she hated the thought of leaving. This was the house she'd grown up in. The only one she had strong memories of. She looked at the doorway that led to her bedroom. Though Shorty was rarely home to enjoy the master bedroom, Becky had never taken it as her own. She'd preferred the smaller room off the kitchen where she'd slept as a child when she and her parents had first moved into the house. Sometimes at night when she was lying awake in her bed, she would imagine that she could still hear her mother moving around in the kitchen. She'd close her eyes, sure that she could smell chocolate chip cookies baking in the oven.

A tear slid down her cheek and she brushed it away. So many memories, she thought sadly. And so many regrets.

With a sigh, she rose and set the hat carefully on the table. But she didn't have time for weeping, she told herself. She had chores to do still.

At least for another couple of days.

The first arrangement of flowers arrived at noon. The second arrived shortly after one. The deliveries continued throughout the day, marking each hour, until every available surface in the Rusty Corral's kitchen was filled with a profusion of color and blooms.

Becky set the last arrangement—three dozen baby pink roses—on a burner on the stove—the only remaining space left in the small kitchen—and plucked the card from among the fragrant blooms. The card was signed simply "Woody," as had every other card.

"This has got to stop," she muttered and headed for the phone. She picked it up and quickly punched in his number. She waited through three rings, then heard his answering machine click on.

"Hello. You've reached the Golden Steer. I'm not here so leave a message."

She rolled her eyes at the no-nonsense recording and waited for the tone. "Woody, it's Becky," she said, after hearing it. "Listen, the flowers are nice, but—"

There was a clattering noise, a curse, then Woody's voice. "Don't hang up. I'm here."

Her fingers tightened on the receiver at the sound of his voice, her heart squeezing painfully in her chest.

"So you like 'em, huh?" he asked.

She could hear the smile in his voice, the almost boyish

pleasure, and had to lock her knees to keep from surrendering to it. She squeezed one hand at her temple. "Yeah, they're nice, but this has got to stop."

There was a long pause, then he said, "Why? I thought you wanted to be romanced?"

She squeezed her eyes shut to hold back the tears and drew in a long breath. "I never said that."

"But—"

"Listen, Woody," she said, knowing she had to end the conversation quickly. "The only thing you're accomplishing is making Dee Dee rich, so stop sending the flowers, okay?" Ripping the receiver from her ear, she slammed the phone back on its base. A split second later, there was a knock at the door.

Pressing her fingertips at her temples, she drew in yet another breath, then squared her shoulders and headed for the front door, prepared to tell Dee Dee herself that she could quit making the deliveries. But a man stood on the front porch, not Dee Dee. She peered at him through the screen door. "What can I do for you?" she asked suspiciously.

"Are you—" he glanced down at his clipboard, then back up at her "—Becky Sullivan?"

"Yes."

"I have a delivery for you. You'll need to sign here." He held up the clipboard and pen.

Hesitantly Becky pushed open the screen door. "What's the delivery?"

He handed her clipboard. "Just sign on line eleven," he said, passing her the pen. He drew a small package from the pocket of his jacket and exchanged it for the clipboard once she'd signed her name.

"Have a nice day, Miss Sullivan," he said and turned and headed for his truck.

Becky let the screen door close slowly, staring at the small package she held. There was no logo, no writing whatsoever on the package to indicate its source, but something told her that it was another romantic offering from Woody.

Sinking down onto one of the packing boxes in dread, she peeled off the tape on one end of the package, and shook out the box enclosed. She opened the lid and found yet another box, this one velvet and with the name of a jeweler with a New York City address.

With trembling fingers, she thumbed up the lid. An ivory card lay inside.

One for each ear. They're the color of your eyes. Woody.

Afraid to look, but unable to resist the temptation to do anything else, she lifted a corner of the card. She gasped, her eyes going wide. Two large emeralds sparkled up at her from a satin bed. She snapped the lid back down, squeezed her eyes shut, then lifted it again, unable to believe what she'd seen.

But the emeralds were still there, staring up at her like the eyes of a cat from a bed of plush satin.

Not cat eyes. They're much too pretty to be compared to something as common as a cat.

Tears filled her eyes, blurring the stones, as she remembered Woody's words.

She closed her eyes again, pressing the velvet box against her breasts.

Oh, Woody, she cried silently. *Why are you doing this to me?*

Forrest snatched the sling-back shoe from the top of his desk and stuffed it into his jacket pocket as he stormed from his house. Every woman likes flowers, he told himself. That's why florists have such a booming business on Valentine's Day and Mother's Day. Hadn't his mother always gone all sappy-eyed when he'd thought to send her flowers on special occasions? Hadn't his own father worked his way back into his mother's good graces by sending her roses after they'd had a spat?

He climbed into his truck, flipped on the headlights and revved the engine. Poems were written about women going weak-kneed when they received flowers from a man, he told himself as he sped toward the highway. Hell, entire plots of movies were based on just such an event!

He flew past Windmill Hill without even seeing the landmark. Becky was different from most women, he had to admit, but she wasn't *that* different. He wheeled onto the lane that led to the Rusty Corral and passed beneath the sagging sign that arced above it. He didn't know what her game was, but he was growing a little weary of trying to figure it out. He wanted to get married, dammit. And she wasn't cooperating one bit.

He braked to a stop in front of the house and was jogging up the porch steps before the door slammed behind him. He rapped his knuckles against the screen door, then pressed his nose against the screen's mesh. The living room was pitch-black but a light was on over the sink in the kitchen.

"Becky!" he called loudly. When he didn't hear a response, he jerked open the door and stepped inside. He tripped over something and swore. Fumbling for the light switch by the door, he finally found it and flipped it on.

"Damn," he whispered as he stared at the tightly wrapped packing boxes covering the floor. He swallowed hard and forced his gaze up. "Becky!" he called again, his heart racing.

He started toward the kitchen, weaving his way down

the narrow path the boxes created. "Becky? Where are you?"

He braced his hands on the door frame and stuck his head inside the kitchen. The scent of flowers hit him full force. Roses. Tulips. Delicate gardenias. Maybe he had overdone it, he thought belatedly. But he honestly thought he was giving her what she wanted.

Seeing a light beneath her bedroom door, he stared at it a moment. Though he'd been in her house a thousand times or more over the years, he'd never once seen the inside of her bedroom. He crossed to the partially open door and pressed his ear against it, listening. "Becky?" he said uncertainly. He gave the door a nudge and it swung open on creaking hinges.

The light that had drawn him came from a lamp on the bedside table next to an old iron bed. An oak wardrobe that looked as if it had come to Texas on one of the first wagon's headed west stood against one wall. There were two boxes on the floor, one sealed and with one with its flaps open, and a straight back chair angled beside the bed.

But no Becky.

He stepped inside the room, feeling like a burglar, or at the least a Peeping Tom, but was unable to contain his curiosity. A quilt was spread over the neatly made bed, its colors reminding him of a summer sky, soft blues and billowy whites. Pillows cased in white were propped against the iron headboard. On one post at the foot of the bed hung her battered hat. On the other a soft cotton gown.

Two steps was all it took to cross to the bed. A bare stretch of the arm to finger the soft cotton. Simple, he thought, and as unassuming as the woman who wore it. He dropped his fingers from the cloth and looked to his right. The wall was covered with pictures and an odd assortment of items, kept in place with tacks pressed into the faded wallpaper. He stepped closer, squinting in the dim light to better see.

There was a picture of him, taken on the day he left for boot camp. Another of him, shot at the airport the day he returned home a civilian. He stepped closer, moving his gaze from picture to picture. He was in nearly every one.

He lifted his hand to a scrap of paper and pulled it from the wall to read and recognized his own handwriting.

To Becky. Love, Woody.

He frowned trying to remember the occasion, the gift to which it had been attached, but couldn't. Pushing the tack back into place, his hand brushed a dried rose, its petals crumbling at his accidental touch. Fearing she'd know he'd been snooping, he tried to straighten the flower and discovered a ribbon tied to its stem with something written along its faded length.

Woody gave me this to me on July 4, 1984.

Nineteen eighty-four? She couldn't have been more than fourteen or fifteen, at the time. And why had he given her a rose? He tried to think back to the year. He would've been twenty, and in his junior year at college. He frowned, rubbing at his temple, trying to remember.

And then it hit him. His parent's twenty-fifth wedding anniversary. There'd been a huge party at the Golden Steer. People had come from all over the state to help his parents celebrate the event. He remembered going to the kitchen in search of a knife to cut the cake and had found Becky there, sitting at the breakfast bar alone.

When he'd asked her why she wasn't out on the patio with everyone else, partying, she'd said that she felt out of place because everyone else was all dressed up. He'd laughed at her insecurities and plucked the flower from an arrangement on the kitchen counter, and stuck it through one of the buttonholes on her shirt, telling her that now she was as dressed up as everyone else.

And she'd saved that rose all these years.

He backed up a step and·sat down on the edge of the bed, his knees suddenly too weak to hold him, and stared at the wall of memories.

She'd loved him, he thought, emotion spinning through his head. All these years she'd loved him and he'd been so blind, so wrapped up in himself and his own life that he'd never even noticed.

Becky bent down and wrapped her arms around the new foal, picking him up to hold him in her arms to begin the bonding process. "Such a beautiful baby," she murmured, rubbing her cheek against his still damp coat. The mare swung her head around and butted her nose against the colt's side. Becky chuckled softly. "Getting even, are you, for all those times he was bumping around inside you?" She set the colt down at his mother's side, holding on to him until she was sure he had his hooves beneath him. He immediately stuck his nose beneath the mare's belly, searching for her bag.

Becky laughed at the greedy sucking sounds he made when he found a teat. With a sigh, she moved to the mare's head. "You did good, mama," she said, rubbing the horse's velvet nose. "You did real good."

"Colt or filly?"

Becky tensed at the sound of Woody's voice, then resumed her rubbing. "Colt."

"Have you named him yet?"

She lifted a shoulder, keeping her back to him. "No. I figured you'd want to name him."

"But you've always named the foals." She heard the gate open, then close, and Woody's muffled tread on the soft bed of shavings.

"Not this time," she said, then tensed again when she felt the warmth of his chest against her back. His hand appeared on the mare's face next to hers and began to rub.

"Any problems with the birth?"

"N-no," she stammered, finding it difficult to breathe with him so close. "She'll make a good brood mare for you."

"For us," he corrected.

Becky closed her eyes against the yearning that squeezed at her heart. "Don't, Woody, please," she murmured. "I told you. I can't marry you."

"Can't, or won't?"

She dropped her hand from the mare's face and turned away, putting distance between them. "Same difference."

"No," he said, turning to watch her as she picked up the veterinary supplies she'd had on hand during the birth. "Can't means there's something stopping you. Won't means you're just being stubborn." He folded his arms across his chest. "The 'can't' no longer exist, since there's no fiancé to keep you from marrying me. So I guess that just leaves 'won't' and you're just being stubborn."

"Think what you like," she said, weary from arguing with him. "The fact is, I'm pulling out tomorrow."

"Where are you going?"

She lifted a shoulder. "I don't know. Probably to Riodoso, for a while at least."

"What's in Riodoso?"

"Who," she corrected, "not what." She rolled up the

supplies in the canvas bag she kept them stored in and secured it with a strip of leather. "Shorty's there."

Forrest looked at her in surprise. "Shorty? You're still speaking to him after what he did?"

He watched her cheeks flush with embarrassment. "He's still my father," she mumbled, as if that explained everything.

And for Becky, he supposed it did. He only hoped that she could forgive him as easily. He followed her out of the stall and into the small room where she kept her supplies. She hit the light switch and a bald bulb on the ceiling popped on, filling the room with light.

He braced a shoulder against the door frame and watched her as she tidied the room, replacing the equipment. He saw the dark circles beneath her eyes, the puffy red rims, and knew that leaving the Rusty Corral was hard on her. He hoped, selfishly, that he might be at least partly responsible for her sadness.

"What if you didn't have to leave? What if you could stay on at the Rusty Corral?"

She whipped her head around to look at him, and he would swear that he saw hope flare in her eyes. Then she ducked her head and wiped a hand along the counter, whisking away imaginary dirt. "The ranch belongs to someone else now. The owners will be here tomorrow to claim ownership."

"The owner is already here."

She turned her head slowly to look at him. "What are you saying?"

He reached into the inside pocket of his jacket, pulled out the deed and held it out to her. "Here," he said. "See for yourself."

"You bought the Rusty Corral?"

He nodded toward the folded paper. "See for yourself."

Nervously, she wet her lips and wiped her hand down
her thigh before taking the deed from him. She shook it
open and held it to the light. He watched her eyes move
across the page, scanning, then they shot to his.

"My name's on this deed," she cried in a hoarse whisper.

"Yep," he agreed with a nod of his head. "It sure is."

"But how?" She turned her gaze to the deed again as
if to make certain her name was really there.

"I tracked down the man who held Shorty's note."

"You bought the Rusty Corral?"

"In a matter of speaking."

She quickly folded the deed back up and held it out to
him. "Then your name should be on the deed, not mine."

"I didn't buy it," he said. "I won it in a poker game."
When she tried to force the paper into his hands, he lifted
them above his head, refusing to accept it. "The ranch is
yours," he argued, "as it should be, and it's in your name
now, so you don't have to worry about losing it ever
again."

Setting her jaw, she stuffed the paper into his shirt
pocket, then flipped off the light and stalked from the
room.

He stared after her, wondering what he could possibly
have done to make her mad this time. "Becky!" he
shouted, following her. "What is wrong with you? I just
gave you the deed to your ranch. I'd think you'd be jump-
ing for joy."

She wheeled to glare at him, her face mottled with fury.
"I don't want your charity, Forrest Cunningham. I can
take care of myself." Spinning back around, she strode
angrily for the house.

Forrest stared after her a good two seconds, then took out after her. "Gawldangit, Becky Lee!" he cried. "Wait just a darn minute." He grabbed her by the arm and spun her around to face him. "I've had it up to here," he shouted, making a slash through the air at eye level, "with your damn pride."

Her chin shot up. "Well, that's too bad, because my pride is all that I've got left."

He closed his eyes and let his head fall back, striving for patience. How was a man supposed to argue with a statement like that? Becky Sullivan had more dignity in the tip of her finger, than most folks could claim in a lifetime. But there had to be a way to give her back her ranch without damaging her Texas-size pride.

Slowly he lowered his chin to meet her gaze. "Flip me for it."

She quit struggling against his hold to stare. "What?"

"Flip me for it," he said again. He released her to dig a coin from his pocket. "Heads or tails?"

She backed away from him. "No. The ranch is yours."

"Hell! I didn't buy it. I won it gambling. And Shorty lost it in the same damn way. What's the difference if you win it back on a bet?"

She opened her mouth to argue the point, then closed it, frowning, when she couldn't come up with a viable reason to offer him.

Knowing the chances of her winning the flip were only fifty-fifty, he sent up a silent prayer that the coin would fall in her favor. "Heads or tails?"

"Heads," she muttered, folding her arms tightly across her chest.

He tossed the coin in the air, watching as it flipped end over end and dropped to the ground between them. He nearly sagged with relief when the face of a past president stared up at him from the ground. "Heads, it is," he said and pulled the deed from his pocket. Taking her hand, he pressed the papers into it. "Congratulations, Miss Sullivan. You're now the proud owner of the Rusty Corral."

She hesitated a moment, then curled her fingers around the papers. "Thanks," she murmured.

"I have something else for you."

She looked up at him warily. "What?"

He slipped a hand into his jacket pocket and pulled out the black sling-back. "I think this is yours."

Judging by the color that rose to stain her cheeks as she stared at the shoe, he figured she remembered the night she'd lost it, and the events that followed.

He took a step closer. "There's a fairy tale about a young woman who loses her shoe and the prince who returns it. They end up getting married. But first she has to try it on and makes sure it fits."

"Don't do this," she murmured and turned away.

He heaved a frustrated breath as he watched her walk toward the house. He counted to ten, then started after her.

She must have heard him coming, because she broke into a run.

He ran, too.

She ran faster.

Weary of chasing her and of arguing with her, he made a dive for her, caught her around the knees and brought her to the ground. Before she had a chance to catch her breath, he was crawling his way up her back and flipping her over. Straddling her, with his knees pressed against her sides, he caught her hands and held them to the ground above her head. He shoved his face up close to hers. "You have to be the stubbornest, most contrary woman I've ever met in my life!"

She thrashed beneath him. "Let me up!"

"No, I'm not letting you up, until you hear me out." He hauled in a deep breath, fighting for patience, and losing. "Here I am, busting my butt, trying everything in the world that I can think of to try to romance you into agreeing to marry me, and you keep refusing my proposals, which doesn't make a lick of sense because I know damn good and well you've been in love with me for years. I saw that wall in your room and that rose that's been hanging there for God only knows how long."

She grew still so fast, it took Forrest a moment to realize she wasn't fighting him any longer. It took another couple of seconds for him to realize he'd just told on himself.

"You went into my bedroom?" she said, the blood draining from her face.

He huffed a breath. "Yeah," he admitted in embarrassment. "But I wasn't snooping," he added quickly. "I was looking for you and thought maybe you were in bed asleep."

She squeezed her eyes shut. "Please let me up."

"*Aww,* now, Becky," he began. But then he saw a tear slip down her cheek. He quickly rolled off her and pulled her up from the ground and onto his lap. "Don't cry," he begged, holding her against his chest. "Please don't. You know I can't stand it when you cry."

Instead of calming her, his words only seemed to make her sob that much harder. He smoothed a hand over her hair, brushing it back from her face as he rocked back and forth, trying to soothe her. He pressed his lips against her temple. "Becky, please," he whispered, desperate for her to stop. "I love you. I'd never do anything to hurt you. You've got to know that."

Her fingernails dug into his skin as she pushed away

from him, lifting her face to meet his gaze. "W-what did you say?" she whispered.

"That I wouldn't hurt you?"

She dashed a hand beneath her eyes, swiping at the tears. "No. Before that."

He frowned down at her. "That I love you?"

"Yes," she said, sitting up straighter on his lap. "That part."

"I love you," he repeated, and watched her face crumple and her eyes flood with tears again. Then she was twisting around and throwing her arms around his neck.

The force overbalanced Forrest and he fell backwards with her sprawled across his chest. But he didn't let go, and neither did she. She just kept squeezing her arms tighter around his neck and wetting his cheek with her tears. Slowly he wound his arms around her, unsure what had brought about the sudden change in her. "I love you," he said again, waiting for her response.

She cried harder, clinging to him as if she was never going to let go.

He braced a hand against the ground and pushed to a sitting position, bringing her with him, then unwound her arms from around his neck and held her out far enough to see her face in the moonlight. "You mean that's all I had to do, was tell you that I love you?"

With tears streaming down her face, she nodded.

He tossed back his head and laughed up at the dark, star-filled sky. "I can't believe this! All that worrying and fretting and running all over the countryside and all I had to do was say three little words?"

She dragged a palm across her cheek and sniffed. "They're not so little."

Laughing, he hugged her. "No, they're not, and they don't come close to describing how I feel about you." He brought his hands to her cheeks, framing her face, and his smile slowly disappeared. "I love you, Rebecca Lee Sullivan," he said, and was suddenly afraid that he might cry, too. "I think I've loved you since the first time I laid eyes on you, but was just too blind to see it." He tightened his grip on her, praying that this time he'd get it right. "Marry me."

"Oh, Woody," she sobbed, laughing and crying at the same time. "I thought you'd never ask."

Epilogue

The Golden Steer was indeed golden on this night. Hundreds of torches joined candles topped with clear hurricane globes to gild the sprawling ranch house's rear lawn in a soft romantic glow. Yards and yards of white tulle draped strategically placed panels of lattice interwoven with ivy and fresh cut flowers, creating an illusion of a gazebo of monstrous proportions, befitting a Texas wedding. A dais erected especially for the ceremony itself rose high enough from the center of the island-size patio to allow each and every guest a perfect view of the bride and groom as they exchanged their vows.

Personally Forrest hadn't seen the need for so much froufrou and would have preferred a simpler and more private ceremony, but his mother had put her foot down, insisting that every woman—Becky included—secretly dreamed of a big, fancy wedding. He'd finally given in and his mother had worked day and night in order to have everything ready within the week's time Forrest had allowed her. Though he'd had to keep a firm rein on his mother to keep her from going overboard, he had to admit that she had succeeded in creating a setting that would fulfill any bride's dream.

Not that he hadn't had a hand in the arrangements himself.

Standing at the edge of the patio, his arms folded across his chest, he turned his head slightly...and smiled smugly. Not a hundred feet away his wranglers manned the smoking pits, barbecuing beef raised and butchered right on the Golden Steer. Behind them, icy kegs of beer waited to be tapped. To their left, members of the band that would play later worked quietly at one end of a portable dance floor, setting up their musical equipment and amplifiers. Around the dance floor tables covered in linen—a concession he'd made to his mother—were set and ready for the feast that would take place after the ceremony.

"Nervous?"

Forrest turned to look at Hank who had stepped up beside him. Though butterflies the size of Hank's private jet were doing dive-bombs in his stomach, Forrest lifted a negligent shoulder. "No. Should I be?"

Hank chuckled. "I sure as hell was on my wedding day."

Forrest stuck a finger between his neck and the collar of one of the new tuxedo shirts Chin-Liang had made for him and let out an uneasy breath. "I just want this damn ceremony over."

"It'll be over soon enough." Hank turned his gaze out over the guests who crowded the patio. "I see you invited Anna."

Forrest followed his friend's gaze to where Princess Anna and her young son stood with Sterling and his wife,

Susan. "Yeah. I thought a party might help take her mind off her worries."

Hank's lips thinned at the reminder of the mission they were all a part of and the one man who still hadn't made it home. "We're bound to hear from Blake soon."

"If we don't," Forrest said in a low voice, "Greg's liable to go after him." He nodded his head toward Greg who stood on the opposite side of the patio, scowling. "He's as worried about his brother as Anna is about the safety of her niece and nephew."

"Can't say that I blame him."

"Forrest?"

At the sound of his mother's voice, Forrest whipped his head around to find her and his father standing behind him. The blood drained from his face at the tears he saw in his mother's eyes. "What's wrong? Is it Becky? Has something happened to her?"

She pressed her fingers to her lips and quickly shook her head. "N-no. There's nothing wrong with her. It's just that…" She dropped her hands and reached for his, forcing a smile to her lips. "You'll see," she said, giving his hands a quick squeeze. "It's time for the ceremony to start."

The butterflies kicked up the pace of their bomb-diving missions as Forrest made his way to the dais. He took his place at the foot of the velvet-lined steps, just as they'd rehearsed the night before, and waited as the harpist filled the night air with the whispered strains of the wedding march.

As if on cue, the guests grew quiet and parted, creating an aisle of sorts that led to the open French doors of the home Forrest had grown up in. Becky stepped into the opening, her hair swept up high and woven with delicate baby's breath, looking like a vision from a dream. The dress she wore was the same one Forrest's mother had worn when she'd married his father almost forty years before. Lace the color of old ivory covered her arms from wrist to shoulder then swept across the bodice of the dress and rose to form a collar high on her neck. Satin of the same color formed a heart over her breasts beneath the lace and hugged her curves, then fell in soft gathers to sweep the tips of her shoes.

Becky Sullivan, he thought, his heart thumping wildly within his chest. His neighbor, his friend…his bride.

He drew in a shuddering breath when her gaze met his and was sure that his heart was going to burst wide open, it was that full of love for the woman who stood before him.

Upon her appearance, startled gasps and whispers rose from the guests, and she tore her gaze from his and looked out over the throng of people who crowded the patio, the blood draining from her face. He saw the tremble of her lips, the panic that widened her eyes, and understood as no one else could her uncertainties. Though he knew he was supposed to wait for her at the steps of the dais, he found himself moving down the aisle toward her.

When he reached her, he took her hand in his, drawing her gaze to him, as well. He squeezed her hand between his. "Rebecca Lee Sullivan," he said softly as he looked deeply into her eyes, "you are, without question, the most beautiful woman I've ever seen."

He felt the tension ease from her fingers and watched the color return to her cheeks as her lips curved in a smile. He gave her hand another squeeze, then drew it through the crook of his arm as he moved to stand beside her. He looked down at her and smiled. "Would you do me the honor of becoming my wife?"

She gazed up at him, her smile turning radiant, her eyes

sparkling like emeralds in the soft light. ''Oh, Woody, there's nothing in this world I'd like better.''

*   *   *   *   *

Don't miss the next installment of the
Texas Cattleman's Club—
*when romance brews between super
secret agent Blake Hunt and the young,
lonely widow Josie Walters in*

SECRET AGENT DAD
by Metsy Hingle

*Coming to you from Silhouette Desire in
November 1999*

*And now for a sneak preview of
SECRET AGENT DAD,
please turn the page.*

The blood in Blake Hunt's veins chilled at the sound of a baby's whimper coming from the backseat of his car. He'd learned a major lesson in the past forty-eight hours—bachelors and babies do not mix. Given a choice, he'd rather face a firing squad than the four-month-old twins strapped in the seats behind him.

"Why couldn't I get a simple assignment—like disarming a band of terrorists?" he muttered. Pressing one booted foot to the accelerator, he sent the sedan speeding down the dark Texas road, barely visible in the heavy rainstorm courtesy of La Nina.

Bone tired from the mission he'd undertaken on behalf of the Alpha mission and his brother Greg, Blake replayed the escape from the palace in his head. Even with his training as a former Cobra, getting the royal twins out of the tiny principality of Asterland where they had been held hostage had not been an easy task. But he'd done it.

He'd rescued the motherless babies and thwarted Prince Ivan's plans to use them in his plot to gain control of the kingdom of Oberland. And in less than two hours, weather permitting, his end of the mission would be complete. They would be in Royal, Texas, and he would gladly turn the pair over to their aunt.

Another whimper cut through his musings. Despite the November cold, sweat beaded across his brow. He lifted his gaze heavenward. Please. Don't let them wake up again. The whimper escalated to a wail. "So much for prayers," he muttered.

"Hang on a second, sugar britches," he soothed, dividing his attention between the blue-eyed babies seated behind him and the storm-ravaged road stretched out before him. He negotiated the sedan around another curve and swore as a fist of wind came at him and nearly tossed them off the road. Gripping the steering wheel, Blake fought to steady the car while he braced himself for the second baby to join its twin's protests. As if on cue, the other baby began to howl and the wails continued in chorus. Blake still didn't know which was worse—the nerve-wrenching cries of the twins or driving through the worst rainstorm to hit west Texas since Noah had piloted his ark.

Sighing, he darted another glance at the duo with the healthy lungs seated behind him. An unexpected warmth spread through him as he looked at the tiny pair all bundled up in the ugly camouflage jackets he'd put on them in their escape from the palace. Miranda—he was sure it had to be that future heartbreaker—stretched out her little arms toward him.

Blake's heart did a nosedive.

"Shh. It's okay, sugar. Uncle Blake's here." Unfastening his seatbelt, he stretched one arm behind him to stroke her tiny hands with his finger. Despite the contact, she continued to sob. And each one of those pitiful sobs ripped right through him. Nearly frantic, he tried to think what to do. "Pacifiers!" Groping in the diaper bag on the seat beside him, his fingers closed around a rubber nipple. "Here you go," he said, managing to pop it into her mouth.

He was debating whether to stop and get the other nipple for Edward, when the baby stopped crying, and started to doze off. Relieved, Blake directed his attention back to the road and frowned. The weather appeared to be worse now than when he'd started out from the airport where he'd landed his plane earlier. The usually dry gullies were filling rapidly. Never once in his thirty years could he remember weather like this in west Texas, the wide open country he hailed from. But he couldn't stop and wait for it to blow over. He *had* to get home—to Royal—tonight and complete his mission with his safe return to the Texas Cattleman's Club.

Another glance at the backseat revealed the twosome were asleep. Anger twisted inside him as he thought about Prince Ivan and his attempts to use them. From what he'd learned of the man, the prince would not be a gracious loser. "Don't you worry, little guys. Uncle Blake won't let him get anywhere near you again. I promise."

Rain pummeled the car like fists, making it nearly impossible to see the road. The windshield wipers worked furiously, offering him only split-second views of the road. His thoughts still on the prince, Blake didn't see the shattered arm of a windmill in the road until he was almost on top of it. He whipped the wheel to his left, just missing it. Struggling to maintain control, he began applying the brakes. A blast of wind slapped at the car from behind and sent the sedan skidding sideways across the road. Blake fought to keep the car from flipping over, but there was no way to avoid hitting the low bridge over the creek. He slammed into the railing, and the car pivoted and began skidding down the shoulder. The babies screamed. Blake lurched forward, cracking his head against the windshield before the car came to a halt.

Dazed, blood trickling down his forehead, the frightened cries of the babies pierced his fogged senses. The twins! He had to get the twins. Fighting pain and the darkness that threatened to engulf him, Blake shoved against the door. It opened, and he fell to his knees in mud and water. He tried to stand, but the wind slammed him back against the car. His head struck the door, and pain exploded in his skull. His vision blurred. Clutching his head in his hands, he slumped to the ground, unaware of his wallet falling beside him, of the wind tossing the black billfold down toward the creek and into the rushing water.

And as the rain beat down over him, Blake succumbed to the beckoning darkness.

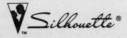

If you enjoyed what you just read,
then we've got an offer you can't resist!

Take 2 bestselling love stories FREE!
Plus get a FREE surprise gift!

Clip this page and mail it to Silhouette Reader Service™

IN U.S.A.
3010 Walden Ave.
P.O. Box 1867
Buffalo, N.Y. 14240-1867

IN CANADA
P.O. Box 609
Fort Erie, Ontario
L2A 5X3

YES! Please send me 2 free Silhouette Desire® novels and my free surprise gift. Then send me 6 brand-new novels every month, which I will receive months before they're available in stores. In the U.S.A., bill me at the bargain price of $3.12 plus 25¢ delivery per book and applicable sales tax, if any*. In Canada, bill me at the bargain price of $3.49 plus 25¢ delivery per book and applicable taxes**. That's the complete price and a savings of over 10% off the cover prices—what a great deal! I understand that accepting the 2 free books and gift places me under no obligation ever to buy any books. I can always return a shipment and cancel at any time. Even if I never buy another book from Silhouette, the 2 free books and gift are mine to keep forever. So why not take us up on our invitation. You'll be glad you did!

225 SEN CNFA
326 SEN CNFC

Name _____ (PLEASE PRINT)

Address _____ Apt.# _____

City _____ State/Prov. _____ Zip/Postal Code _____

* Terms and prices subject to change without notice. Sales tax applicable in N.Y.
** Canadian residents will be charged applicable provincial taxes and GST.
   All orders subject to approval. Offer limited to one per household.
   ® are registered trademarks of Harlequin Enterprises Limited.

DES99   ©1998 Harlequin Enterprises Limited

THE FORTUNES OF TEXAS

*Membership in this family has
its privileges…and its price.
But what a fortune can't buy,
a true-bred Texas love is sure to bring!*

Coming in November 1999…

Expecting…
In Texas
by

MARIE FERRARELLA

Wrangler Cruz Perez's night of passion with Savannah Clark
had left the beauty pregnant with his child. Cruz's cowboy
code of honor demanded he do right by the expectant
mother, but could he convince Savannah—and himself—
that his offer of marriage was inspired by true love?

THE FORTUNES OF TEXAS continues with
A Willing Wife by Jackie Merritt,
available in December 1999 from
Silhouette Books.

Available at your favorite retail outlet.

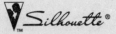

Silhouette®

Visit us at www.romance.net

PSFOT3

Don't miss Silhouette's newest cross-line promotion,

Four royal sisters find their own Prince Charmings as they embark on separate journeys to find their missing brother, the Crown Prince!

The search begins in October 1999 and continues through February 2000:

On sale October 1999: **A ROYAL BABY ON THE WAY** by award-winning author **Susan Mallery** (Special Edition)

On sale November 1999: **UNDERCOVER PRINCESS** by bestselling author **Suzanne Brockmann** (Intimate Moments)

On sale December 1999: **THE PRINCESS'S WHITE KNIGHT** by popular author **Carla Cassidy** (Romance)

On sale January 2000: **THE PREGNANT PRINCESS** by rising star **Anne Marie Winston** (Desire)

On sale February 2000: **MAN…MERCENARY…MONARCH** by top-notch talent **Joan Elliott Pickart** (Special Edition)

ROYALLY WED
Only in—
SILHOUETTE BOOKS

Available at your favorite retail outlet.

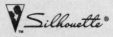

Visit us at www.romance.net

SSERW

SILHOUETTE®
Desire

COMING NEXT MONTH

#1249 HEART OF TEXAS—Mary Lynn Baxter
Man of the Month 10th Anniversary
Businessman Clark Garrison had come home to River Oaks for
one purpose—to make a profit. But that was before he met
Dr. Sara Wilson...and realized his profit would be her loss.
Would Sara still want to be his partner in life once the truth
was revealed?

#1250 SECRET AGENT DAD—Metsy Hingle
Texas Cattleman's Club
Widow Josie Walter had never wanted to get close to another
man again, but she couldn't help believing in happily-ever-after
when handsome amnesiac Blake Hunt landed on her doorstep—
with four-month-old twins. But once regained, would Blake's
memory include a knowledge of the love they'd shared?

#1251 THE BRIDE-IN-LAW—Dixie Browning
His father had eloped! And now Tucker Dennis was faced with
the bride's younger niece, Annie Summers. Annie only wanted
her aunt's happiness, but when she met Tucker, she couldn't help
but wonder if marrying him would make *her* dreams come true.

#1252 A DOCTOR IN HER STOCKING—Elizabeth Bevarly
From Here to Maternity
He had promised to do a good deed before the end of the day,
and Dr. Reed Atchinson had decided that helping pregnant
Mindy Harmon was going to be that good deed. The stubborn
beauty had refused his offer of a home for the holidays—but
would she refuse his heart?

#1253 THE DADDY SEARCH—Shawna Delacorte
Lexi Parker was determined to track down her nephew's father.
But the man her sister said was responsible was rancher
Nick Clayton—a man Lexi fell in love with at first sight. Would
Nick's passion for her disappear once he found out why she was
on his ranch?

#1254 SAIL AWAY—Kathleen Korbel
Piracy on the high seas left Ethan Campbell on the run—and in
the debt of his rescuer, Lilly Kokoa. But once—*if*—they survived,
would Ethan's passion for Lilly endure the test of time?